I'm in the middle of the Festival, looking at this guy, and this is when I see the girl with my hair. She is across the street, too. She is behind a wall of people. Her head pops into view and then bobs out of sight. A flash of red. Now, for a second I see her face. I can't tell what she looks like, but her skin is too white. The redhead's skin. It freckles, sunburns, and peels. I know all about it.

Men and women on horseback suddenly charge down the street. Then for a second the street is clear and I look for the other redhead. She is gone. I feel an ache of disappointment. The parade starts. But I keep looking for the redheaded girl....

Also by Charlotte St. John
Published by Fawcett Juniper Books:

FINDING YOU

SHOWDOWN

RED HAIR

Charlotte St. John

FAWCETT JUNIPER • NEW YORK

This book is dedicated to my sister, Claire.

RLI: $\dfrac{\text{VL 5 \& up}}{\text{IL 6 \& up}}$

A Fawcett Juniper Book
Published by Ballantine Books
Copyright © 1989 by Charlotte St. John

Library of Congress Catalog Card Number: 89-91310

ISBN 0-449-70320-7

Manufactured in the United States of America

First Edition: November 1989
Third Printing: February 1990

SECTION I

Emily

CHAPTER ONE

I see myself uptown today.

I see my look-alike across the street. She looks like me because of her hair. It is the same rotten color as mine. Shredded carrot.

Before this happens, when I am still in bed this morning, I remember school is out for the Festival. I jump out of bed. I pick out a loose pullover and my new pants. I go to the breakfast table, sit down between my parents, and stuff a doughnut in my mouth.

Mother is talking to Dad when I sit down. She leans around me and keeps talking to him. She is describing a float she designed for the Festival parade. I already know about it, so I am bored. She reaches over and tries to pat my uncombed hair into place.

"Nobody in the world has hair like yours, Emily," she says to me.

She is wrong, but I don't know this yet.

Mother studies me. She knows I want to look good today because our town will be crawling with guys from other places. Some of them will be college guys.

She curls my hair around one of my ears. "The toner makes the difference," she says. "What a color we got with the beige toner!" She leans around me again and says to Dad, "I would kill for hair like this."

Dad gets up and goes to the stove. He has his back to us. I know what that means. It is his way of disagreeing.

He is making the coffee. The old-fashioned way. First he boils it. Next he sets the pot off the stove and cracks an egg. I watch him pry the eggshells apart. *Plop*, the egg insides fall into a bowl. With a flourish he drops the empty eggshells in the coffee pot. This is supposed to "clear" the coffee.

He turns around. "I don't see why you two work so hard on Emily's hair. It looked just as good before you toned it down," he says.

"I wish you wouldn't do that, Wesley," Mother says. I figure she is referring to the eggshells in the coffeepot. I want her to talk some more about my hair. When a subject is this horrible, I can't get enough of it.

But the minute Mother speaks, Dad reacts. "Why do you wish I wouldn't do that?" He yanks at his bathrobe sash. It is already tight around his middle.

Mother is cool. "Because." She nibbles a slice of fresh pineapple. With one finger, she picks at a frosted, chocolate doughnut then pushes it away. She gives Dad an accusing glance. Or maybe she is just trying to see him. She is nearsighted.

My mother's eyebrows are arched and black. She stares, or glares, out from under them. She says its unhealthy to wear glasses all the time. To a stranger she might look unfriendly. But if you asked her, she would probably say vampires are nice people suffering from an iron deficiency. She gives everybody a chance.

Glaring at Dad, she says, "Sometimes, I get a jellyfish thing in my mouth. Out of the coffee cup. I know it is egg white." She shivers her shoulders, twitching her Japanese kimono.

"Then we will strain your cup hereafter." Dad feels around in a drawer and brings out a sieve. He strains a cup of coffee and hands it to my mother. "Greater love hath no man."

Greater love hath no man, I mouth silently, looking away. He can't help it, I tell myself. He's got a nineteenth-century tongue.

We are eating the doughnuts and scattering the crumbs everywhere when Dad demands, "Tell me, Emily, what's wrong with red hair? I had it. My father had it. His was just the color of yours."

I love it when he gets wrought up about me. I frown

hideously and prepare to snarl at him when my eyes catch the wall clock.

I jump up. "I've got fifteen minutes to get to town!" I am dashing for the hall. "I'll see you guys later."

"What's the hurry? I thought I was going with you." My mother's voice.

I had hoped my mother and I would go to the Festival separately. I am meeting my new boyfriend, Kyle, on the square. I turn around.

Mother gets out of her chair, one hip bumps the table, and Dad's quick hands grab the coffee cups.

"I'm meeting Kyle," I tell her. I think she won't want to go with me when she knows. She doesn't like Kyle. He is the only person in the world she doesn't like. But I am nearly sixteen and allowed to choose my friends, so in a way her not liking him doesn't matter.

I tell her again, "I am meeting Kyle."

"No problem." Her kimono billows out behind her tall figure as she follows me down the hall.

My mother is a fine person, but she can be pretty insensitive. Like now. I remind myself she is not my real mother. Of course I have always known this. My parents told me a long time ago my own mama died when I was a baby, and Dad married Mother when I was just learning to walk. But there were years when I pretended Mother was my natural mother. This was easy to do. She really loves me. Dad says she married him to get me.

She is the first person I remember. I have always wanted to be like her. Everybody admires her. But I can't forget the other mother I never knew. In my mind I call her "Mama."

At times like this . . . this is when I remember Mother is not my natural mother. And she and I are different kinds of people.

Should I give up trying to be like her? Or try harder?

Now I wait at the front door.

"Here I come." Mother appears, fastening a parrot-shaped earring on one ear. "Emily and I are leaving," she yells toward the kitchen. Dad comes down the hall, tightening the sash around his middle until it looks as though it might squeeze him in two. Mother looks down at him (she is a head taller) and strokes the lapel of his bathrobe. "The parade passes right below your chambers, Wesley. Will you look out and wave to me?" What my mother calls my Dad's "chambers" is his office suite. Dad is a judge. DISTRICT JUDGE WESLEY PETTY is written on his door.

My parents will always be sweethearts, I am afraid. It is embarrassing.

Dad's little, muscular face with its ropes of wrinkles looks pleased. I can see he is happy to be asked to hang out of his office window to wave to Mother.

Mother gets in behind the wheel and starts us off with a soft *swoosh* of the Cadillac. We cruise uptown and around the square. Our town was named Fern for Dad's grandmother, a woman who kept chickens and sold eggs. The town was built around the square a century ago in Central Florida away from a lot of the Florida hype. We get our share of strange faces, a few older couples come down for the winter, plus there is the annual fall influx of college students who attend the college on the edge of town. But our year-round population is about seven thousand, including the migrant workers.

I see a band of college students now roaming noisily across the stage of the outdoor bandstand. Along the street a crowd is gathering for the parade.

We don't see Kyle, so we cruise around the square a second time. The crowd overflows into the streets, making it hard for cars to get through. Mother drives slowly, nodding at people she knows.

"Isn't that Michelle?" Mother asks. Mother smiles broadly and says, "Our Citrus Queen."

I look where she is looking and see Michelle. My best friend. She is walking like she's been practicing in front of a mirror. Very languidly. Swiveling those tiny hips. She is going to writhe in agony having babies someday, as I see it.

"Yeah. That's her all right," I agree. Michelle turns her lean face in our direction, sees us, and waves. That face too . . . okay, it is beautiful in a carved-to-sharp kind of way. Same color as her hair, tanned and golden. And that hair . . . obedient. She can make it look trashy in an instant. Or classy.

Michelle and I are both nearly sixteen, but I look fourteen and she looks twenty.

"You want me to stop?" Mother asks.

"Go on, Mother. I'm looking for Kyle, remember?" I wiggle my fingers at Michelle, and we drive on. Mother puts on her good-sport face. She really wishes I would get along better with Michelle because Michelle's mother, Francine, is my mother's best friend. That is why Michelle and I have been stuck with each other all through school: if our mothers hadn't been friends, I don't know . . . Michelle is okay. But I wonder if there isn't some other girl more like me. Someone I might have chosen for myself.

"Kyle isn't here," Mother says. "And I've got to take the car out of the parade route. They're getting ready to rope it off."

"Please go around just one more time," I say. She noses the car slowly around the square again. We are both silent. Finally I say, "Why don't you like Kyle?"

"Did I say I didn't like him?" Mother asks. She turns her large, gray eyes on me. I always feel about two years old when Mother looks right into my eyes. I pull myself together.

"Do you like him?" I ask.

Mother hesitates. "I guess I don't know Kyle. Why doesn't he come to the house to see you? So your dad and I can get to know him?"

"Nobody does that anymore. It's dumb. What's wrong with meeting him here?" Will she win this round? The possibility makes me reckless. "You think he's a nerd, don't you?"

"I hate that word, Emily. I wish you wouldn't use it. No, I don't think Kyle is a nerd. From what little I've seen of him I'd say he's shy or maybe inarticulate . . ."

"Not everybody talks as much as Dad, Mother. Not everybody wants to." I am feeling intense about this and almost don't see Kyle. He is standing in the square peering over heads. I hail him. His face brightens when he sees me. Will Mother think he is fat? I look him over. Sometimes he wears fat-looking clothes. But today he is dressed okay.

"Hey, stop." I am getting out of the car before it stops. Mother glares hard until she sees him. When her eyes focus on him, she smiles and waves. Then she gives me a concerned glance.

I relent. "I'll be watching for your float. Both your floats," I tell her. I'm on the sidewalk. She drives off.

"Want me to tape you?" Kyle asks.

I see he is dying to use his new video camera. It is slung by a strap over his shoulder. "You'll get a chance to practice on the parade. Come on. Let's get something to eat." It's ten o'clock, none too soon. I am always hungry.

We push through the crowd toward the courthouse parking lot where we hear a country band playing. Square dancers are in the parking lot, yipping and kicking and flipping hats and skirts. It is contagious. I realize I feel good. I get serious about our search for food, and soon we spy a row of vendor tents. We pick out luscious bits to munch: hot popcorn, chicken wings, and pita sandwiches stuffed with avocado and sprouts. Our mouths are bristling with sprouts as we go looking for our friends. The first person we see is Michelle.

"Oh! You're back. I thought I saw you leaving with your mother," she says.

"Leaving? I was arriving."

"But . . . you were already here. An hour ago. I saw you. I called to you, but you walked off, and I couldn't find you." Michelle's eyes begin to move away from us. She is ogling a group of college boys. I glance over at them.

I catch one of the guys looking at me. A blond kid. I've never seen him before. He must be a freshman, I think.

I murmur, "I just got here. You must have seen someone else."

She frowns. Still boy-watching, she says, "It was you. I could spot your hair anywhere. . . ."

We both lose interest in the subject. The guys take our full attention. They are returning our looks. I become aware of Kyle. He has finished his sandwich and is taping the street where people are jockeying for space on the curbs.

I whisper to Michelle. "Who is that guy?"

"Cute, isn't he?" she says. "I'll find out and get back to

you." She looks at her watch. "Got to go." She has to change into her queen clothes.

The guy moves like a basketball player. Not that tall, though. His crowd is crossing the street. He looks back at me once more. We study each other. Dare each other. I like his attitude. I watch him disappear in the mob.

This is when I see the girl with my hair. She is across the street, too. She is behind a wall of people. Her head pops into view and then bobs out of sight. A flash of red. Now for a second I see her face. I can't tell what she looks like, but her skin is too white. The redhead's skin. It freckles, sunburns, and peels. I know all about it. I know how she feels when people say "Aren't you lucky to have red hair!" It's embarrassing to have red hair. Everybody stares at you.

I get one more glimpse of that hair. The rotten-orange, shredded-carrot mop. I guess she hasn't heard about the miracle of beige toner.

Men and women on horseback charge down the street. I glance at Kyle. His head is jammed against his video. The riders wave banners to signal the start of the parade. A wagon train follows. It is driven by men in overalls and straw cowboy hats. I can see their loafers below their pants' legs. They rattle past, shouting "Gee!" and "Haw!" and throwing their hats in the air.

For a second the street is clear, and I look for the other redhead. She is gone. I feel an ache of disappointment. The parade starts. But I keep looking for the redheaded girl.

CHAPTER
TWO

My mother's float is the first one. It is the Pioneer Museum float. Mother is supposed to ride on it because she is president of the local historical society. I look for her, but all I can see is the back of a big, black iron stove.

The float moves forward very slowly. The people lining the street start clapping. My mother's head comes into view. Then her shoulders. Now I see the rest of her. She is flipping pancakes. She is wearing a calico dress, a wide apron, and a sunbonnet. With a twist of her wrist, she flips a pancake in the air and catches it. She does it again. The parrot-shaped earring swings madly. She forgot to take it off! If I had helped her put on her costume, I'd have got the earring off. She sees me and smiles. I hold my ear and point to her. Her eyes get wide, and she grabs the earring. Off it comes with a yank. We laugh at each other.

The rear end of the float is coming into view. I see Grandpa sitting in a rocking chair. He is playing his fiddle. "Listen to the Mockingbird" flows from it sweetly.

He lifts the fiddle bow, waves it at me, and brings it down against the strings with a lurch in the tune that makes us both laugh.

I punch Kyle, who is still photographing Mother and Grandpa. He looks up at me.

"Mother's float is next," I tell him.

He raises a hand and points toward the Pioneer float sailing majestically down the street away from us. His mouth opens.

"I got her. I got the pancake business," he says.

"No, no, I don't mean that float. Look!" The float that my mother designed noses slowly toward us. It is followed by a loud burst of enthusiastic applause. She took a prize on this one last year. This is her Home-Decorating Service float.

Kyle starts filming again. The float is beside us now. It is even better than last year's, I think. It sounds like a barrel of chipmunks. The squeaky voices are singing "Heigh Ho, Heigh Ho, it's off to work we go . . ." Sleek puppets are racing around on their tracks in their designer jumpsuits, putting up drapery, hanging wallpaper, and arranging indoor greenery. It is all color and motion.

This is the perfect float. From the perfectionist.

At her job Mother is the best in the area. Everybody says so. Our house is the biggest house in town, but until Mother remodeled it, it was just an old-fashioned Southern Colonial. Now, Dad calls it a showplace because Mother shows it to her customers. Once a prospective customer sees it, a contract is guaranteed.

Every color and fabric in it either coordinates or "provides a striking contrast." Or a "deliberate element of surprise." For example, Mother put a lot of surprises in my bedroom.

In the middle of my floor is an ottoman the size of a round bed. Big enough to play chess on. Then there is my bed. Is it a stage? Is it a miniature theater? If it is a bed, and I sometimes wonder, it should belong to somebody like Lady Macbeth. She could sleep on it by night and act on it by day. Or hide in it with the curtains drawn, and argue with herself in complete privacy.

Like the rest of the room, the bed is done in a "family of colors," all kin to pearly gray (which won't "offend" the color of my hair) and a "suitably subdued" apricot (which will soften it). The "striking contrasts" are a navy blue. A navy blue polyurethane desk and chair. A navy blue throw rug. The rest is coordinated. All except me. Of course, I am lucky to have such a room. As Michelle says.

* * *

I look around for Michelle but don't see her.

Kyle is taping busily. When he comes up for air, I say "Thanks."

He packs his camera away, and we watch the rest of the parade.

There are a lot of agricultural floats. Pigs go squealing by. Chickens in crates peck and squawk, and goats bleat. The citrus industry floats come by last. One has a throne shaped like a giant orange cut in half. Michelle sits on it looking vaguely uncomfortable. Maybe an orange seed is poking her in the backside. Maybe I am jealous.

Just before the end of the parade the crowd begins to break up, and I tell Kyle I have to go find my mother and go home for lunch.

"When do you want to see the tape?" he asks.

On an impulse I say, "Bring it over tonight, and we'll run it by Mother and Dad on the big TV." Dad has a wall screen almost as large as the screen in a regular movie theater.

A smile spreads over Kyle's broad face. His eyes sparkle.

"I'd like that," he says.

I have been putting this off, this bringing him to the house. I never know how my parents will react to a new friend. They are satisfied with my old friends. Of which I am . . . not sick. But I need something more in my life. I don't know what.

I haven't told them Kyle is the college president's son. I hinted that his mother was in prison and his father trafficked in pornographic films.

They think I am totally trouble-free. What have I ever done to worry them? I am always where I say I am going to be. I am always home on time.

Actually my parents are born worriers. If I gave them a real problem, they would disintegrate.

Kyle is still smiling. I think he is loosened up by my invitation to come over tonight.

"Guess what, Emily!"

"What?" I wait. Kyle is slow. He is quick mentally but slow to respond.

At last he says, "I entered the Festival Competition. With a song. Want to hear it?"

I shudder. Why do people spill their guts to me? No, I don't want to hear it. But I have to nod, don't I?

Kyle clears his throat. "It goes like this:

> There's a dead alligator in the pool, in
>> the pool,
> And if you want to ride him, you're a
>> fool, you're a fool,
> Cut off his tail, put the pieces in a pail,
> And send 'em off to alligator cooking
>> school."

We stare at each other. We are both in a state of shock. Why did he do this to us just when we were beginning to feel comfortable together?

Kyle snorts. It is a laugh. An effort to be casual. Too late.

I think the guy is crazy. Just when you think you can trust one, he confides in you, some pukey thing. Like once this guy told me he swallowed his pet grasshopper . . . no, it was a cricket, one of those big, stinking, Chinese crickets. We were in sixth grade. He had brought the thing to school. When the teacher asked him what was making all the noise, he swallowed it. He said a cricket foot got stuck in his throat and was there for hours, all through lunch. He ate anyway.

I hate some guys. Maybe all of them. But everybody associates with them, so I have to start.

This song is as bad as the cricket, as I see it.

"Go on," I say heartlessly.

"That's it," he mutters.

What can I say? "I hope you win."

Silence. I know Kyle is smart. Maybe a genius. I am trying to decide if he is also an idiot.

"I'll bring the tape over tonight," he says. He gives me a sullen look and adds, "But I won't stay long." He picks up his taping gear and heaves into the crowd.

I think the guy is angry. What did I do?

When I get home about one o'clock, I find my mother stretched out on the patio. "There's chicken salad in the fridge," she says, glaring at me nearsightedly. Her glasses are on a table beside her. Her hair is dripping.

"You had a swim?" I ask her, pointing at the pool. She nods wearily. "You okay?" I ask.

"It's my feet. I better get used to it. The Festival is just getting started."

"The puppet float was great, Mother. You're going to win again."

When my mother smiles, I can see how pretty she might have been if she didn't have acne scars.

"Keep saying it. It gives me strength." She sighs. In a minute she says, "Emily, I want to try lemon juice on your hair. Francine puts it on Michelle's hair. Every time I see that child, her hair looks lighter. Did you notice? I think we could lighten yours the same way."

"Why does Michelle walk like that? She didn't used to walk like that," I say sulkily. I don't want to talk about Michelle.

I remember something and get excited.

"Guess what I saw across the street during the parade? Hair exactly . . . *exactly* . . . like mine."

Mother is still smiling. But the smile is going. She looks doubtful.

"You saw . . . ?"

"Hair the same, exact color of mine. Without the toner."

She pushes up on an elbow. "What did you see?" she asks.

This seems like a stupid question to me. I try to answer another way. "I saw a girl about my size with hair the color of mine. I didn't see her up close. Next time I looked she was gone. So I can't prove it. You'll have to take my word for it. Think of it, Mother, there is another head of hair in the world exactly like mine.

Mother shakes her head. "No way." She falls back in her chair. Her arm goes lax.

"Don't take it so hard." I laugh. "You can't fix everybody's hair. But you've still got me. If the lemon doesn't work, we'll find something else." I don't laugh this time.

After a weird silence, during which I wonder if I am getting tired of all this fuss about my hair, Mother says, "We've got to stop this obsession with hair."

After a minute or two I look over at her again. Her head is back, and her mouth is open and a tiny snore pops out of her nose.

I hear the door behind me open. It's Dad. I put my finger to my lips, but it's too late. Mother sits up, dazed. Dad looks like he is bursting with news.

CHAPTER
THREE

"I need to talk to your mother, Emily," Dad says.

His eyes are snapping, but his voice is low. Very controlled. These are bad signs. Or good signs. It's hard to tell. He can look and act this way when he is announcing the approach of a hurricane. Or the ice cream man. This look works well for him in court. The lawyers can't psych him out.

I say, "Sure, I'm out of here." I leave the lovebirds alone on the patio and go inside. I pull the bowl of chicken salad out of the fridge, grab a fork, and take the stairs two at a time. I am thinking my father's big news is about a court case. Dad has to sentence people accused of crimes, and sometimes this keeps him awake nights. It affects Mother, too.

I crouch at the head of the stairs on the second floor under a window overlooking the pool and patio. I am stuffing salad in my mouth when my mother's voice rises up to me.

"Maybe she is right. She is growing up. We should give her more space. You should, too."

Their voices lower. I look out. Dad holds out his short arms, and my tall mother goes into them. Somehow they don't look ridiculous. He pats her back. She smooths the hair on the back of his head. I move away from the window. There is too much love oozing back and forth between them for me to watch.

I missed the big news, of course. All I know is it is about me. I like that. It sounds good. I don't remember asking for my space. I planned to do that on my sixteenth birthday next month. But who's arguing?

I go to my room.

As I pass my dresser, I pick up a mirror. I crawl up on my stage-bed and sit, lotus-position. Dancers love to sit this way. It keeps our legs flexible. I look in the mirror to consult with myself. What can be done about my appearance? When you think about it, everybody's face is a little peculiar. All these holes. Holes that work hard. I count the holes. Seven, if you count my ears. Air goes snuffling in and out of your nose twenty-four hours a day. Your nose never quits. Your eyes and mouth work like crazy, but they get to rest. I think your ears have it the easiest.

I push my hair back and look at my ears. Still there, still huge. Like the Buddha's ears. Way too big. Fat earlobes. I pull my hair back over these two obscenities.

My nose is perfect. I've looked at it in profile, and it is perfect from that view, too. My eyes are gorgeous. Blue. Intelligent. Expressive. Be honest! A little loony. But I don't have those yellow eyelashes that come with red hair. I roll my eyes up and say "Thanks." Only God could have wrought this miracle of black eyelashes and dark eyebrows. I think it was his way of compensating for the hair. The Petty hair.

My natural mama was dark. She was Mexican. Judging from one little snapshot I keep in my desk, I didn't get anything from her. No, that's not true. My coloring is so different, it is hard to see a likeness, but I think I got her cheekbones. And her big mouth. And there is something about my eyes: they aren't as slanty as some Mexicans' eyes, but they turn up at the corners.

Like my mama's eyes.

It looks odd on me.

Mother, the only mother I know, says someday I will like this exotic look.

She is delighted with my "development." I have big breasts. Way too big for a skinny fifteen-year-old. I wear a fat thirty-six bra. Next to my hair, I hate my bust the most.

When Michelle comes over, I hide my big bras on my top closet shelf. I do this because Michelle rummages

through my chest of drawers every time I leave the room.
Once I threw a handful of tacks in the drawer to discourage
her.

I went to the bathroom and came back. She was into my
top drawer up to her elbows.

"Look at this!" she exclaimed.

"What are you doing in my drawer, Michelle?" I asked.

"Picking these tacks out for you. Look!" She showed
me a handful of tacks. I punched her, not too playfully. We
had a minor quarrel. That was last week. Today at the
parade we're back to normal. She's a friend, I guess. But
not the kind you can love like a sister.

I had a sister. A twin. She died with my mother. That is
hard to believe because I feel as though she is with me
every day.

Somebody taps on my bedroom door. "Come in," I say.
Michelle comes in. "Your mom said you'd be up here."

I start to tell her she looked good on the float, but she
rushes on: "I found out who the blond guy is. I couldn't
wait to tell you."

Suddenly I am glad to see her.

She scrambles up on the bed. "His name is Dean. He's a
freshman at the college. And he's from Charleston, S.C."
She is as bouncy as a puppy waiting for its strokes.

"Dean," I say. "Michelle, you did good." If she had a
long tail, she'd waggle it. This beautiful, popular girl who
looks like we all want to look and who has a great-looking
jock boyfriend . . . why does she try so hard? She already
has it all. Doesn't she?

She runs a hand through her silky hair. It is hanging in
wide waves today. Merely gorgeous beyond belief.

"How did you find out?" I ask.

"Broderick told me." Broderick is her boyfriend.

"How did Bro—?" I begin. She interrupts.

"He asked him. He went up to the blond guy and asked
him because I said you wanted to know." She cocks her
face on one side and shimmers goldenly at me.

"Oh, no!" I cry. I bend over and push my face down,
down into my pearly-gray comforter. I make a big fuss, but
I am glad to get the guy's name.

We enjoy a loud, sweaty quarreling session, about Michelle's big mouth and my ingratitude, then I ask her what she thinks of my new boyfriend, Kyle.

"I want the truth," I say.

"He's nice. I like him a lot."

"Get real," I say.

She throws her arms out imploringly. "That is what I really think about Kyle," she says. She clamps her mouth shut. I know it's over unless I take action.

"And this is what I really think about Broderick: there is, you know, hope."

Michelle is so polite! She sits there, looking attentive. Puzzled but attentive.

I continue: "In our own area we have several fine dog-training schools. They could teach him how to chew with his mouth shut. How not to scratch his armpits in public. Or spit on the sidewalk. They can cure burping, mumbling. Adjusting his crotch. They do wonders down at Fido's Friends. Or Peppy Puppy. Or Just Dawgs. Any one of those places could fix a case of the slobbers."

Michelle is sliding off the bed. The golden face is red now.

I go on: "If that lump on his Neanderthal forehead develops a bit, he might give the hound dogs a run for their money. We're talking years from now, of course. But you've got to start somewhere." I say all of this in a voice of sweet reason.

"Kyle is a nerd. And he's fat. And he is unpopular. Where did you find him anyway? Under a moldy computer . . . that died of slime mold out in the swamp?" She is yelling.

"Gotcha!" I scream. I rock back and rip out a huge laugh. My long legs come loose from under me. I kick both legs in the air and gurgle with laughter. I throw both the pillows toward the ceiling. One flies out of its case and meteors off across the room, leaving a comet tail of feathers that fall softly over us.

Michelle creeps up on the bed on her knees. Her face is total distortion. (I have done this to her so many times!) Then a smile breaks out. She laughs as she slides backward onto the floor. She rolls on my "contrasting" navy blue throw rug. Back and forth. All the way over, clutching her middle and shrieking.

I sit up, perfectly sober, and announce, "Kyle is coming over tonight. To get to know my parents. Oh, Michelle, what am I going to do?"

She sits up and considers the question.

"Are you going to skip the Citrus Show this afternoon?" she asks.

"Absolutely. How can you stand it? Facts of the citrus industry. You have to go, don't you?"

"Speaking of which . . ." She looks at her watch. "Just be nice tonight. Don't show your fangs. You can be nice. Once long ago I observed you being nice." She slips out of the door, pleased with herself.

Kyle arrives. On the dot, of course.

CHAPTER
FOUR

My parents and I have finished supper and are stacking dishes in the dishwasher when I hear the door chimes.

I go to the door and there is my fat nerd. He is carrying the tape he shot this morning.

"Hi," we both say at once. We laugh. But he seems grim.

I lead him into the kitchen to meet my parents. Introductions rattle some guys but not Kyle. He extends his hand like a grown person and murmurs the proper words. I can see undisguised approval creeping across my mother's face. Dad's expression is always harder to read. He is looking watchful but not displeased.

I'd feel more sympathy for Kyle if he weren't enjoying himself. That's part of his nerdism: he is more at ease with adults than with teenagers.

Kyle offers to set up the TV room. Once in there, he marvels at the size of the screen. Actually I think this is why he came over, not to see me but to see it. We don't talk. He keeps his back toward me.

"Are you mad at me?" I ask.

"You could say that," he says.

"Why?"

"You acted like my song was roach meat."

"I said it was good." I did say that!

He turns and looks at me.

"You've got that eyebrow, Emily. The left one. When you are lying, it jumps. You didn't know that, did you?" he asks. His scowl goes, and he smiles ghoulishly.

My hand flies up to my face. I feel the telltale eyebrow.
"Look, I didn't mean . . ." I begin.

"Don't try, Emily. It's too late." He turns his back on
me again.

I feel so bad. So small. I say, "I'm not good at writing
myself." I stop. What am I trying to say? "Maybe that's
why I didn't appreciate the song."

He turns around again. He studies me. "Nobody can do
everything. I've seen you dance. You're good at that." He
bends over and adjusts the tape.

"You have?" I was in a dance recital last month. He
must have seen that.

He finishes with the tape and sits back on the floor. In a
second he puts his arms around his knees. I sit down on the
floor, too, opposite him. Something happens between us.
A shift of some kind. It feels better.

I say simply, "I apologize, Kyle."

For a second he looks doubtful. I wait. But I am very
busy. I shoot him through and through with my eyes. Over
and over I make my eyes tell him I'm sorry.

He gets to his feet as he says lightly, "Apology ac-
cepted."

This is not going to be easy; I can see that.

My parents come in, all smiles. Mother says, "Roll it,
Kyle. We're ready." They sit in the two big armchairs facing the screen, and I sit on the floor in front of them.

The first images are rocky, but in a second we get a
steady view of the street scene. Good grief! There is my
blond guy, Dean, going across the street. My heart jumps.
Dean is turning his head to look back at me.

I wasn't wrong. That is a special look. Right now I'm
giving a special look back to him. He disappears in the
mob on the other side of the street.

I hear a sound behind me. It's Dad.

"What's going on?" I ask, turning.

Mother says, "Nothing. Dad wants an apple. Go get
one, Wesley."

Dad gets up and goes out. In a minute he returns with a
bowl of apples and passes them around. I take one and
look at the screen. I almost miss her. The girl with my hair.

"There she is!" I yell. "Look, everybody, there's that

girl I told you about. Did you see her?" She is gone now. "Did you see her hair?"

"Did you see her, Wesley?" Mother asks Dad, polishing an apple on her sleeve.

"Look, Kay, here comes the Pioneer float. There . . . isn't that you under the sunbonnet?" Dad points at the screen. "You did a good job, Kyle. Mrs. Petty and I are indebted to you."

I give up. Nobody saw the redheaded girl.

I watch for Mother's next float, and soon it comes into view. Kyle got a close-up of two of the puppets, the two hanging drapery. We all watch excitedly.

"Kyle, you're good," Mother says. "For your reward, we have homemade ice cream. Chocolate and vanilla. And all kinds of fruit to put on top." Mother watches for Kyle's reaction. He is smooth, this kid. He smiles and ducks his head. It's like an agreeable little nod.

"You didn't have to do that," he says. But I can see him salivating.

The four of us sit around the breakfast table heaping our bowls full of ice cream, whipped cream, mangoes, guavas, and strawberries. We eat like we are in church . . . silently, devotedly. This stuff is good. I am hoping it makes up for the trashy way I have been treating Kyle.

Afterward I think Kyle and I will watch something stupid on TV, make fun of it, and feel superior, but he says he has to go. I walk out to the street with him. We are under a lamp post, so I can see him when he says, "I've got a question for you, Emily."

That makes me nervous. I say, "What?"

"Why did you start with me? Why did you meet me in the park today? Why did you ask me over here tonight? If you don't like me, if you don't like the person I am, why bother?"

Kyle has a square jaw. It juts out.

I close my eyes and think about what he's said. It makes me remember why I started with Kyle. I remember I admired him. He was always the smartest guy in the class. Not in a wimpy way, not just to show off how much he studies. I have never seen the guy study. What he does is read all of his textbooks the first week of school and remember everything in them all semester. Is that studying? Whatever, I admired it.

But more than that, I liked Kyle. He wasn't wordy, but we talked. Every time our eyes connected, we understood each other. A good feeling. I could say something to the guy in a few words, something complicated, like in the Chemistry lab (where I'm smarter than he is), and he'd get it. I guess you could say we communicated.

I say, "I wasn't allowed to date until this year. Then, when I was allowed, I didn't want to start. Until I got to know you in Chemistry lab. I wasn't afraid we wouldn't talk. I figured I could date . . . as long as it was you."

It is his eyes that keep me going through this long speech. Kyle's eyes keep me trying to explain. Also he keeps up those agreeable little nods. This is encouraging. And, best of all, he is looking more friendly.

"I didn't want to admit to anybody, or even me, that I liked you. It's hard. My friends watch to see . . . if a girl likes a boy, they watch to see if he likes her, too. Sometimes he doesn't, and it's embarrassing. I would feel like a fool if that happened to me," I say.

"I like you," he says.

"I didn't know that, for sure. I was afraid to show I liked you until I was sure you liked me. I pretended . . . even to myself, that you weren't so great. Because I was afraid to hope you and I . . ." I can't think of how to say it.

"You are full of surprises, Emily," he says, shaking his head. He seems to think it over. "Thanks for being honest. That helps."

"Friends?" I ask, reaching for his hand. He takes my hand in his and gives it a squeeze.

"Friends," he says. "Are you going to the Gopher Races tomorrow?"

"Absolutely."

"I'll come by for you. Want to go on our bikes?"

I go inside, feeling pretty good. I get to the door and hear my parents voices. Low, murmuring. I do it again—I eavesdrop.

All I hear is Mother whispering, "Wait, I think she's coming."

CHAPTER
FIVE

It is the second day of the Festival. Mother has to leave early to take some Christmas wreaths to the Pioneer Museum. She is in charge of the museum's Christmas sale.

Still in my pj's, I help her load the wreaths in the back of the station wagon.

"I like this one," I say, holding up a giant wreath made of dried grapevines and pinecones and lots of red berries.

"Do you want it for our front door?" she asks.

I look at her, surprised.

"I thought these wreaths were made to raise money for the museum," I say.

"You're right. But I could buy it. I think it's right for this house. You've got an eye for such things, Emily," she says. She runs a hand across her forehead.

"You okay?" I ask.

"Fine." She gives me an unusually bright smile. "Have a good time at the Festival, my dear. Let me know how the Gopher Races turn out."

I wave her off and go back inside to dress. It is turning cooler, so I choose a deep blue shirt and a wine-colored sweatshirt. I pull on a pair of khaki fatigues and sneakers. Dressed now, I walk in front of my wall mirror.

I hope I see Dean today. I look better today than I did yesterday.

The thought of the guy makes my heart jump.

I am bent over brushing my hair when Dad knocks on my door. I can tell it is he: dad always raps three times.

"Come in."

In comes his head. His white hair above his bright pink skin makes him look like a healthy ghost. Or like Santa Claus. But he is small and hard-muscled. And while his expression isn't grim, it's not what you could call jolly.

I throw my head back, which gets the hair off my face so I can see him. He has found a seat on the edge of my desk. He looks very neat in his gray suit and navy blue tie.

"How are you getting along in your Driver's Ed course?" he asks.

"I'm the best," I say, tying my hair back.

Dad's eyes gleam. A small smile twitches his mouth.

"You're doing well, are you?"

"Yep." My hair is fixed. I am ready to go. I pick up my purse. Nobody moves. I can see Dad wants to hear more, so I say, "I was the only one who could parallel-park on the first try. My teacher says I've got a good eye. Or aim. She says it's because I'm a dancer." I execute a sloppy pirouette for him, coming down with a thud. "She says it's because I'm well-coordinated."

"Baloney! It's because you are a Petty."

We smirk at each other. Our smirks are identical. We don't look exactly alike, but our expressions are often the same.

"Yeah. We Pettys are b-a-a-d," I say.

More smirks. I come up on the toes of my clumsy sneakers again and point a toe.

"How would you like a car for your birthday?" Dad asks.

I fall, just barely catching myself on the bedpost. I hang on, then pull myself up.

"A car? For me?" My voice croaks. I sound like a bullfrog. "You always said I couldn't have a car until I was eighteen." Whose side am I on anyway?

"If you learn to drive well, I could change my mind." He stands up. "Can I give you a lift to town?"

"No, thanks." My voice is still shaky; I hurry on. "Kyle is coming by on his bike. We're biking to the park for the Gopher Races."

"Then I'll be off. Think about what I said. Get a good grade, and we'll talk car."

* * *

I tell Kyle immediately.

"So, what's the big surprise? All you rich kids get cars," he says.

We are pedaling toward the edge of town to the park. Two blocks away we are already slowed by a mob. Cars, bikers, and people on foot clog the road. A cloud of dust rises. We have to get off our bikes and walk them the rest of the way.

"My folks have never . . . they don't do this sort of thing. They don't throw money around, period." We push through the Gateway and park our bikes among the others.

"They got everything for free? The tennis court, the pool, the Jacuzzi? The condo—there's got to be a condo at the beach—no? . . . in the mountains, then? I thought so. They just wave a magic wand, right?"

I forget I am trying to be extra nice to Kyle today. "I don't think I like your opinion of my family," I say.

He laughs softly. "I didn't mean it as an insult. Your old man earned it. I admire that. I'm just saying . . . if I had punched your background into a computer, a car would come upon the screen as your most likely sixteenth-birthday present. I'm just saying I'm not surprised." He gives me a studious look. "I like all kinds of people. You don't have to be poor to win my heart. Speaking of poor, wait until you meet Scurvy Dog." Kyle looks around as though searching through the crowd for somebody. "He's here somewhere."

"Scurvy Dog?" I ask. We are walking toward the open field where the races will be held. Kyle is getting ready to answer when he yells and moves away from me.

"Hey. You got a big one." He is running. I look ahead and see a guy lifting a tortoise out of a box. The tortoise's head and feet are drawn up inside its shell. I come up beside Kyle. Both guys glance at me.

"This is Scurvy Dog. Scurvy, this is Emily," Kyle says, weaving his hands back and forth between us. The strange guy nods at me, then both guys gaze at the tortoise. It looks like a solid rock. There is an emblem painted on its back. The emblem looks like a peanut.

"Feel him." Scurvy Dog puts the animal in Kyle's hands. "Heavy, isn't he?"

I can't stand the way guys jock it up when they get together. I push between them.

"Gimme," I say. Kyle passes the animal to me. I scratch his back. I am thinking along these lines: woman's tender touch will relax him. Nothing happens.

"He's sick," I offer. "You've got yourself a sick gopher turtle," I tell the guy.

"Maybe, maybe not," he says. "Let's see how fast he will accelerate from zero." He puts the tortoise on the ground.

Nothing happens.

"Fast, isn't he?" I say. The guys look at me reproachfully. "I'll be over at the lemonade stand," I tell Kyle. To Scurvy, I say, "Remember, steroids are illegal." This gets a laugh. Scurvy Dog is good-looking, especially when he laughs. A Mexican kid with beautiful skin and a great body. I wonder who he dates? Then I remember: the kids in my high school don't date the migrant workers' kids. He has to be a migrant workers' kid. The few Mexican kids we have in school are from migrant families. Why does he call himself that awful name? It's like the names the local kids, the rough ones, actually call the Mexican kids. I stop in my tracks. Maybe that's it. Maybe he's saying to the world, "I beat you to it."

I start on, head down, and almost bump into Broderick. Michelle is behind him.

"Ask for a glop of fruit slushy. It makes the lemonade better," Broderick advises. His Neanderthal brow is dropping bits of ice onto his nose. He must have pushed his head into his glass. The ice on his nose is melting. Maybe he will inhale it and drown.

"Where's Kyle?" Michelle asks.

"With Scurvy Dog. And a gopher turtle that won't move."

Michelle frowns. "Where have I heard that name?"

"The Mex kid," Broderick tells her. "Don't you know Scurvy? He's the computer whiz. The teachers call him in when their computers get stuck."

"He's a Mexican kid?" she asks.

"That's right." Broderick moves his head closer to hers. "He lives in one of those shacks out on the highway. They all live out there. My dad says the city ought to raze those shacks. He says they're 'unsightly.'"

Broderick's dad is the town's mayor.

"Scurvy Dog looks all right to me," I say.

"Oh, sure. He's not deformed or anything. He gets along well with all the guys. But my parents say I can't have him over. They're afraid he'll give me something. They say those ghetto kids carry strange germs. Nothing against the Mexicans. We all carry germs. But they're susceptible to our germs. Our germs kill them off like flies. And we're susceptible to theirs."

"Baloney!" As soon as I say it, I hear how it sounds. Like my father. The difference is my father would know how to follow up. I don't. I can't explain why I feel so sure Broderick's folks are wrong.

Broderick laughs at me.

I've got to learn how to argue with guys like Broderick. I am as disgusted with myself as I am with him.

Michelle steps between us. "I'm having some kids over tonight for pizza. You and Kyle will come, won't you?"

"I'll ask him," I tell her. We are jostled by a group of people who push up to the stand and order drinks. I move to one side. I get separated from Michelle and Broderick. I glance back toward the park entrance where I left Kyle.

I feel the hair rise on the back of my head.

Someone is staring at me.

How long has she been watching me?

A woman. Small, slender. Tanned-looking skin. Aztec cheekbones and lips. Hair in a braid around her head.

She stands under a tree about fifty feet away. Her glasses flash blindly. Although I can't see her eyes, I know she is looking right into mine.

I stare back. Neither of us moves.

With a wave of motion and sound, some college guys rush toward the lemonade stand. They come between me and the woman. They surround me. Their shouting deafens me. When I am able to step to one side to look for the woman, she is gone.

Dean, the blond boy, the guy of my dreams, is standing in front of me. My mind goes blank. I completely forget . . . whatever it was I was looking at.

CHAPTER
SIX

"Hello, again," Dean says.

"Hi," I squeak.

He is wearing white. White everything. Pants, shirt, sweats, and sneakers. He is taller than I thought. He is looking down at me. He looks gorgeous.

"I was afraid you weren't coming. I'm glad you could get away. Here's the comb you left in my car." He hands me a small comb, the kind you stick in your hair to hold it back.

What is he talking about? Is this the way college kids talk? Is this supposed to be funny? Am I missing something? I stare at the comb in my hand.

To be on the safe side, I say, "I worked it out."

He takes my hand and squeezes it. "Did you miss me?"

Good grief! "Uh, yes," I say. I wonder if my left eyebrow is jumping. Missed him? Been in his car?

He takes my arm. "Come on. They're getting ready to race." He hasn't taken his eyes off my face. How do we walk without looking where we are going? We stumble forward. I don't fall down.

We get to the end of the field where the kids are lining up their tortoises. We stop at the starting line, and Dean's hand slides down my arm to my hand. Which he holds.

Again his blond head bends close to mine. "Want to make a bet?" he asks.

"Sure," I say.

He pulls change out of a pocket and buys a couple of tickets. We are betting on tortoise number five, name of

Queen Elizabeth. We get as close as we can to Queen Elizabeth's racing lane, and Dean thumps the queen on the back. The animal's head darts out, then draws back inside. The queen's owner, a girl about ten, assures us Elizabeth is greased lightning on the runway, but to me Elizabeth looks dead.

Dean stands close, our sides touching all the way up and down, and we discuss our animal's chances. I am thinking a tortoise race is a great icebreaker. Suddenly Kyle is on my other side. What now?

"Want to place a bet on Scurvy Dog's animal, Peanuts?" he asks, out of breath.

Dean looks at Kyle. Surprise is all over his face. Kyle doesn't seem to notice Dean.

"Uh. You do it," I say. This is getting out of hand.

Kyle moves off to trade his change for tickets.

"Who was that?" Dean asks, dropping my hand.

"Kyle? He's a guy at school."

"You didn't come with him, did you?" he asks. His eyebrows are pulling together.

"I, uh . . . I came with him. Is that what you mean?" Sometimes I am so dumb!

"Excuse me." Dean backs away like I've got chicken pox. He looks hurt. Like a little kid. "I guess I didn't understand you," he says.

I don't know what to say. I don't know what he's talking about. But I don't want to challenge him. Things are messy enough as it is. And let's face it, I haven't got the nerve.

At my silence his look turns into disgust. Maybe scorn. He walks off. I watch him find his buddies on the other side of the racetracks. He doesn't look at me again.

Somebody sets off a firecracker, and the race begins. Or doesn't, depending on which tortoise you are looking at. There are twelve lanes, and only three of the animals move out from the starting position. The three that move crawl along slowly, holding their dusty heads up. Now two more start. One is Peanuts, Scurvy Dog's tortoise. He soon passes the others. Kyle and Scurvy Dog cheer him on. Queen Elizabeth starts but falls asleep. Several animals won't start. One starts the wrong way and tries repeatedly to climb back over the starting rail to the safety of a gopher hole.

That's the one I feel like. I want to crawl in a hole. I don't understand what happened with Dean. He said a lot of puzzling things. He acted like I came here to meet him and then walked off with someone else. One thing is clear: He hates me now.

Peanuts is ahead. Michelle and Broderick are running alongside the track, screaming encouragement to a tortoise named Pee Wee. This is the biggest animal in the race. He crawls from side to side with lots of energy but won't go straight down the runway.

Kyle and Scurvy Dog are talking intently to Peanuts. He is still in the lead but has slowed down. The guys have moved to the end of the lane and are calling him. Scurvy Dog holds up a peanut, and the tortoise blinks. He rises up on his clawed feet and hurries to the finish line.

Peanuts wins!

A wild roar erupts. There are cheers and groans. People pick up their tortoises and put them in boxes to take them to the woods and let them loose. The runway is prepared for the next race.

Kyle comes up to me. "Great, huh?"

"Great," I agree.

Scurvy Dog is taking Peanuts out to pasture. He passes us, waving a blue ribbon.

"Congratulations!" I say.

"Next time . . . trust me!" he says, smiling. He takes me in for the first time. "You guys want to celebrate with a hot dog? Wait right here. Be back in a minute." We watch him free Peanuts at the far end of the field.

"It takes a while to get to know him," Kyle says. "He's got an interesting background."

"What do you mean?" I ask.

"His father died in jail. This guy, his dad, was called 'Scurvy Dog.' That's why Scurvy here took the name. To honor his dad." Kyle looks proud.

Scurvy Dog is back, and we follow the smell of onion relish to the hot dog stand.

I am heaping the relish on my dog when I ask Scurvy, "Is your mother here today?"

He looks a question at me. "Yeah. She's over there." He motions toward the tree where I saw the Mexican woman. "Why?"

"I just wondered," I say. Scurvy watches me, suddenly wary. Our eyes connect and lock. "Scurvy, what's it like where you live? Is it dirty?" I can't help myself. I have to know.

Kyle gives me a horrified look.

Scurvy looks at Kyle. He wags his head. He turns back to me. Our eyes connect again. "Why do you think that?"

Kyle closes his eyes and waits.

When I don't answer, Scurvy says, "Sure, of course. And when the rats come, we skin them and eat them before they get tall enough to open the door to our house."

Kyle giggles.

All together we munch down on our dogs. The onion relish stings our tongues, noses, and eyes, and we squint at one another. We chew.

"I am half-Mexican. Did you know that?" I ask Scurvy. I want him to know I am really interested in where he lives. I don't want him to think I'm just a curious rich kid.

He stops chewing. He has a big wad of bun inside one cheek. He can't speak, so he points at me. He swallows. He looks accusingly at Kyle. "You didn't tell me."

Kyle says, "I didn't know." Kyle is looking at me with new interest.

Scurvy says, "You could have fooled me. I mean, the red hair doesn't fit." After a pause, he adds, "But now that I know it . . . I can see . . . something. What did you say your name was? Your last name?"

I tell him.

He flinches like I've hit him in the face.

CHAPTER
SEVEN

Michelle sashays toward us. "Don't forget tonight. Be there around seven. Come hungry."

"Where?" Scurvy asks.

Michelle hesitates, then she blurts out, "My house. Two hundred Country Club Road. Bring a girl if you want to," she tells him. She smiles at him, then at us. "Anybody seen Broderick?"

"Me. I saw him. Somebody was carrying him out to the field. In a box. Don't try to catch him. He was wild to return to his burrow," I say.

Kyle and I go to his house, which is next to the college campus. His dad has told us to come by for sandwiches on our way to the tennis tournament. We drop our bikes on the lawn and go around to the back of the house where Dr. Jay Marcus is working in his lily pool. His friend, Dr. Patti Pryne, is helping him. Dr. Pryne teaches at the college, too. So does Kyle's mother, the other Dr. Marcus. Kyle's parents are divorced.

I figure when my parents find out the Marcuses are from California and Kyle's dad is dating a black professor, they will be downright thrilled. They'll be relieved nobody in Kyle's family is in prison and eager to socialize with a mixed couple. There aren't many in our town.

And Dr. Pryne. She is not just any woman. She is gorgeous. An athletic person with curves.

She sees us first.

"Hi. Come help." She waves a long, wet lily stem at us.

"We're putting in red water lilies." She reaches down into a tub and pulls up a red water lily. It looks great against her skin. She holds it for us to sniff as we get close enough. "Not much scent, is there?" she says.

"Where are the sandwiches, Dad?" Kyle asks.

"We'll have to send out. I haven't had time to make them." His dad's face is close to the water's surface. He is peering into the water. "Here he comes!" He jumps backward, and Dr. Pryne jumps out of the pool, splashing us.

"Who?" I don't see anything.

"The eel," Kyle says. "He is small, but he can shock. He's our watchdog. The little kids in the neighborhood are scared of him."

Dr. Marcus laughs. "That's how I keep them out of the water garden. I'm a mean old devil! Hi, Emily."

"Want us to order the sandwiches?" I ask. I am hungry.

"Would you? Make my sandwich a pizza with mushrooms. Phone's in the kitchen." Kyle and I start toward the kitchen. "Get what you want," he calls after us. "Wait! Patti, what do you want?"

We stop long enough to take her order and go inside.

Kyle phones in the orders, and we're sitting at the bar stools at the counter drinking Perrier. Kyle keeps dumping lemon slices in it. I find a fork and poke it into the bottom of my glass to pierce the lemon so I can taste it.

"You're Dad's nice, Kyle." I met his Dad with Dr. Pryne at a soccer game a couple of weeks ago. "He's fun."

"He's a good guy. We get along. I used to live with Mom. In our old house. It's bigger. Has a game room. And a pool. It was a great place to bring kids. You've never been with me to Mom's, have you?"

"Nope. You're lucky," I tell him. "Why did you move?"

"Mom's going to get married again. I figured they'd want to have the house to themselves for a while. I miss that game room, though," he says.

"Do you like this guy?" I ask. "The one your mom is going to marry?"

"Not especially. He's a lot younger than Dad and Mom. Don't get me wrong: if that's what my mom wants, it's okay. But he doesn't understand our ways. He wants to play the heavy father. I'm not used to saying 'sir' every time I want to ask a question. I can't remember to do it. When I forget to 'sir' him, he gets . . . worried. Desperate. He can't handle a man-to-man relationship with me. Do you know what I mean?"

"Not really. But I have to say, I like your attitude. I wish I could be that cool with my parents."

Kyle puts an arm around me. "Don't be hard on yourself. You do all right. Considering what you've got for parents. . . . Hey, wait! I didn't mean that the way it sounds. All I mean is they are both coming from another century. Way, way back, long, long ago. There's nothing wrong with that. It's just a little unexpected. Know what I mean?"

I think I agree with him. My dad is more old-fashioned than my mother. Dad is a throwback to some other time. But he is still special to me. I've always looked up to him.

Kyle still has his arm around me. "You're getting there," he says. "I was childish like you a few years back. . . ."

I look at him angrily and see him grinning.

"Don't talk down to me, fool," I tell him. "Just because you act like some kind of grown-up nerd doesn't make me a child, you know." I move out from under his arm.

"I know I'm immature," he says. "Who isn't? Name somebody our age who isn't."

I put an arm around him. "You're better than some of them. Broderick, for instance."

He cuts his eyes over at me while backing away. "Is that the best you can do?"

I can tell he wants to kiss me. I want to, too. Have I got to say something stupid, something flattering, to get it to happen?

He is watching me warily. "I never know what's in your mind, Emily."

I think: nobody does except Elaine. But that's a crazy idea. Elaine, my twin, is dead.

We are getting nowhere. I put my other arm around him. That gets us close together. His eyes light up.

Our faces come closer. Our foreheads touch, and we stare upward at each other until my eyeballs hurt. Then our noses touch. They slide past each other. I think it is so neat the way noses slide alongside each other. We are kissing.

After we all finish our pizzas, Kyle helps me load my bike into his dad's station wagon. Dr. Pryne is playing in the tennis tournament this afternoon, and Kyle and his dad are going to cheer for her. She is changing into an 1890s tennis outfit, a big, flopping thing. Beautiful! They asked me to go, but I think I'd better report in, so I decide to go home.

We all pile in the wagon with Kyle and me in the seat in the back.

He puts his arm along the back of my seat, and we smile at each other. I think I'm in love.

We are cruising along Meridian Street, nosing through the tournament crowd, when the wagon comes to a crawl. We slow; we almost stop. A city bus in the next lane comes up beside us, and it stops, too.

My eyes stare. I am gazing at my reflection. My reflection in the widow of the bus stares back. I press my nose against the glass of the window of the station wagon. My reflection doesn't do this. It stays where it is. The blue eyes grow wide. The mouth parts.

Something else is funny. The face I am staring at . . . the hair is up under a baseball cap. Only a ponytail of red hair sprouts out from the back of the cap.

The traffic begins to move again. The bus in the next lane falls back as the station wagon moves forward. I stare back. The face stares forward at me. Don't go! I cry silently.

The wagon turns a corner. The bus turns the other way. I watch it as long as I can see it, which is about two more seconds before it is hidden by the cars that fall in behind it.

For a second I was sure . . . this was my twin. Elaine. How ridiculous!

"What are you doing?" Kyle wants to know.

I am turned around. Now I turn back and sit, looking forward again.

I mutter, "I saw something I can't figure out."

CHAPTER
EIGHT

My mother drives me to Michelle's, and I find Kyle waiting for me on the front porch. We knock, but nobody answers the door, so I lead Kyle through the house, out the back door, and into the backyard. Michelle and her mother, Francine, have decorated the big yard with lanterns. They hang over our heads from an invisible wire that goes from tree to tree in zigzags. The breeze sways the lanterns, making our shadows dance around our feet.

Michelle's father, Mr. Mackenzie, owns a chain of pizzerias. He learned how to make pizza from his Italian chefs. He stands by a table loaded with every kind of pizza topping available to the human race. So it seems to me. Behind him is an outdoor oven. He holds a pizza spade. In the oven it goes. Out it comes with a beautiful, lightly blistered giant of a pizza.

Like a pack of wolves several of us attack it, cutting off jagged chunks and devouring them on the spot. Burning our tongues and squalling. A chunk doesn't come off fast enough for Broderick, so he yanks it loose, pulling two or three more slices with it. It all goes inside his mouth in less than a minute.

Mr. Mackenzie watches, awestruck but admiring. He manages to say "Enjoy."

Scurvy, Kyle, and I put fresh slices on plates and sit together on a yard swing. Kids are wandering over the yard in couples and groups. When they pass us, they converge on us, then melt away. We start a conversation with one bunch and finish it with another.

Everybody speaks to us. Some of the smart kids ask Scurvy questions about our school computers. I don't think about it at the time, but later I realize nobody sits with us.

I wonder if Scurvy notices this.

"I couldn't get any of my friends to come with me," he says. "Nobody in my neighborhood would believe I was invited." He laughs, but I don't see how this could be funny to him.

Kyle looks thoughtful. "I'll be out to see you tomorrow," he says.

"Bring Emily," Scurvy says.

"Where?" I ask, but somebody calls Kyle's name. It's Broderick.

"Hey, Kyle. I've been looking for you. Can I use your notes to study for the chemistry test tomorrow?" He hunches over us, looking hopeless. An ape without a tree to climb. Sentenced forever to roam the ground among human beings.

Our swing is in a shadowy nook. I suppose our faces aren't easy to see until you get up close to us. Broderick is standing there looking worriedly from Kyle to me when suddenly he sees Scurvy Dog sitting beside me. He puts his hands in his pockets and backs off several feet.

"Sure. Come over Tuesday night. Scurvy and I are going to study together. We'll help you. I'll get Dad to help you, too, if you need a super tutor," Kyle says.

"Tuesday? I don't know. I got to check my calendar." He backs away still farther, then turns around and walks away.

I don't think Kyle knows what happened here. But Scurvy knows. He looks sober. He studies the ground. Soon after that he leaves.

I dream about being watched. In my dream I am standing alone in an open field. The field is surrounded by trees. Back under the trees I see something move. I can feel . . . I mean, I actually feel the touch of someone's eyes on me. It is scary. The hair on my arms stands up, and my skin tingles.

Then I see her. The dark-haired woman. She steps out from under the trees. She is wearing sunglasses. I can't see her eyes, so I start walking toward her. As I get closer she reaches up to take the sunglasses off.

I am going to see her!

This is when I wake up. This is Wednesday, the third day of the Festival. I've got to get up. While I dress I think about my dream. I know what it means: I will always miss my first mama. Every time I see a Mexican woman, I think of her. Like when I saw Scurvy's mother at the Gopher Races yesterday.

I wish I could have known Mama. I can't help but wish it, but the very thought of such a thing makes me feel disloyal to Mother. My mother has always done everything a mother could do. What more do I want?

Why am I crying?

CHAPTER
NINE

It is cool this morning. If I use the pool today, I'll have to heat it, I tell myself. I find my bathrobe and head for the kitchen. Staring at me from the kitchen breakfast table is a note, propped against the sugar bowl. "Don't forget the clogging demonstration," it says. It's from Mother. She and Dad must be gone already. I look at the clock. How could I sleep so late? Eight o'clock!

I am eating cold bread and butter when the telephone rings. It's Kyle.

"Want to go with me to the barrio this morning?" he asks.

"The what?"

"That's Spanish for the migrant workers' community. Dad is taking one of the college service clubs, the one he sponsors. He asked me along." Kyle pauses. I don't really know what he is talking about, so I don't say anything. He goes on: "It's a chance for us, Emily. To see what college kids do with this Pioneer thing. Dad says they are putting the pioneer spirit to the test, that it should be people helping people. Like in our great-grandparents' day. These kids are going out there to repair roofs, dig irrigation ditches, test the drinking water, work in the stockroom, you name it. What do you think?"

"You can't go," I yell. "This is Wednesday. Have you forgotten the chess tournament?" Kyle is the chess champion in his division.

"Nah! I'm not competing this year. I turned in the old crown. I'm not saying chess is kid stuff, but it just seems

41

. . . unimportant right now. I've got to go, Emily. Dad's waiting in the car. Can we come by for you? Do you want to go or not?"

"I want to go. . . ."

I am surprised. I expected a row of shanties, muddy roads, a garbage pile in a nearby field. I don't know what else but not what I saw as we pulled up in front of the Workers' Exchange.

Everything is neat and clean. Small yards, small frame houses with tin roofs. Clotheslines in back. Clothes flapping in the wind. A goat tethered in a field. No garbage piles anywhere.

I get a funny feeling. Like these are toy houses for children only. This makes me feel like a child again for a minute. I see two dark-haired children playing on a swing set. Some toy chickens . . . no, I mean, some small chickens, about half the size of regular chickens, scratching the ground in a pen behind the children. A white, bright sun comes down. The clothes on the line snap noisily in the wind. I can hear it. But I am still in the car with the windows up. No sound comes through. It's just that . . . I remember that sound!

"Hey, wake up! We're here, Emily." Kyle pulls me out of the backseat of his dad's car. A college van draws up beside us, and college kids tumble out of the sides. There are both guys and girls, all dressed in old shirts and jeans. I don't see Dean. That's a relief.

The college kids get the best jobs, of course. Kyle's dad has grouped us in the stockroom and is assigning kids in pairs. Soon everyone has a job except Kyle and me. The place is emptying fast. Kyle begins to fidget.

"I'm coming to you two now," his dad says. "This room we are in, the stockroom, needs a complete inventory. Can you do it in about an hour?"

We try to look eager, and he leaves us.

We look around. Government issue sacks, big ones, of beans and rice. Drums of powdered milk and dried vegetables. Salt, sugar. Flour. How utterly fascinating! I give Kyle a sour look. I am thinking: I gave up clogging for this!

We do it. I write as he calls out items and weights. We

get through about ten o'clock. Not bad. I begin to feel some satisfaction about this deal. It was a job, and somebody had to do it.

"We're the good guys," Kyle says, smiling. "I know you were bored, but you're a good teammate, Em. Here's what I call a bonus: I can read your writing." He looks at me with those somber eyes. I like the way Kyle looks at me. More every day.

"You did all right, too, for a city boy."

It sounds like I'm not overly impressed, but I am. "Want me to look for a snack?" I ask.

I aim toward the nearest door, and it leads me into the front of the building that serves as the retail store. There are few giveaways here. People pay what they can afford for food and secondhand clothes. Pennies, nickels, dimes. Only the sick or longtime unemployed get things free.

Am I the only one in the store? I look around. I don't see anyone. I can't find a snack machine.

"Can I help you?" a voice asks. I whirl around. There is this really short person, a girl about my age.

"Where is the snack machine?" I ask.

"We don't have one. But here are some fresh-picked oranges. Here, have an orange." She takes an orange out of a crate and hands it to me.

"Thanks, uh, are you going to eat one, too?" I ask.

"Sure." She gets an orange. "Let's sit over there."

I follow the girl to a bench behind the counter, and we sit and begin to peel our oranges.

"I am Ilda Suarez," she says. "In English, my name would be 'Hilda,' but I spell it 'Ilda' so people will pronounce it right."

She must go to the high school. But I don't think I've ever seen her. Or, if I have, I don't remember her. The Mexican kids all stick together. So do the white kids.

"I am Emily Petty," I say.

"I know you," she says.

I am embarrassed. "Yeah? You're not in any of my classes, are you? I'm a junior." I think she must be a freshman or a sophomore. She is so little, maybe five feet two.

"I'm a senior. No, I am not in any of your classes." She smiles at the idea. Like it is a little silly.

I'm surprised. I don't know what to say.

"Everybody says I look young because I'm short," she explains. She finishes her orange and gets up. "Back to work. I hope I finish unpacking these boxes before the bus gets here." I must look puzzled, because she adds, "There's a bus from the north coming in this morning. In the winter the farm workers have to go south to find work. We're expecting several families to arrive in a few minutes on the bus. They will need everything. Clothes, food. Jobs. And a place to stay. Do you want to help?" She begins to open a large cardboard box. I can see the name of the sender on the side of the box. The Episcopal Church. Our church.

Ilda pulls a dress out of the box. It is dark red with a white lace collar.

"Oh! Isn't it beautiful!" She holds the dress up to her shoulders. "Do you suppose it would be wrong of me to try this one on? Maybe, buy it myself?" Her dark eyes are big and round with the question.

"No. Why don't you try it on?" I watch her cuddling the secondhand dress as she disappears behind the screen to change. I hope I didn't sound funny. Or look funny. I don't think Ilda noticed my surprise. That dress was one of mine. An old one I told my mother to throw away. I was tired of it.

Ilda's own dress flies up and falls over the top of the screen. In a minute she comes around the screen wearing the red dress. It is far too long. I am five feet seven. It is a little too tight in the hips. Ilda's hips aren't big, but mine are smaller. It is loose in the shoulders where I am broad. But she looks good. The red color is reflected in her cheeks, and she is smiling.

"Help me, Emily. Zip me up the back," she says, whirling around.

I zip her up. The old zipper wants to catch in the cloth, but I work it up carefully.

"There," I say.

She turns around. Her short fingers go to the lacy collar. She smooths it lovingly. On an impulse I reach out and tie the ribbon sash in a bow in the front. Then I stand back. "Ta Dahhhhh!" I sing.

She laughs at me and marches around the store with her

head in the air and her hands on her hips. "I am an important person," she tells me. "An American ambassador to Mexico. In my most expensive dress."

Her hair is pulled back from her face and held by two combs, one over each ear. She wears gold earrings that glow against her creamy skin. Her nose is pointed more like mine than Scurvy Dog's (his nose is short). Her lips are thin. Is this a Mexican look? I wonder. Then I realize Ilda doesn't look like anybody else. Now that I am looking at her really hard, I see that her face (like Scurvy's) is one of a kind.

Why haven't I noticed her in school? I wonder. I wasn't really looking, was I?

Ilda turns her head and looks toward the stockroom. Quickly she looks back at me.

I don't hear anything. I listen. Then I hear Kyle's voice.

"Okay, Em, but I think you look better without them," he is saying.

When did the guy start to talk to himself about me? I suppose I should be flattered.

"That's my boyfriend, Kyle. Can I take him an orange?"

Ilda has resumed her modeling. She moves in front of a door mirror and sways from side to side. "Help yourself. But first tell me how I look. Tell me the truth. Is this color okay on me, Emily?"

"It's good on you. You look good."

She glances over at me.

"You look really good," I say. I mean it. That color is better on her than on me. "But don't wear it to my birthday party. That's next week, and you're invited." I'm afraid some of my friends would recognize the dress. "This is a dress to wear to church, don't you think?"

I freak out over my stupid explanation, grab an orange, and dash back to the stockroom. Why did I invite this girl to my party? The invitation popped out of my mouth before I knew what I was saying.

I find Kyle cleaning shelves. He has moved a row of cans off the last shelf and is wiping the dust off.

"Phew! Not this way," I say, fanning the dust out of my face. I hand him the orange. He hands me something.

I take the thing, but I know before I look at it what it is.

A small hair comb. A perfect match for the one Dean "re-turned" to me.

"You must have dropped this. When did you start wearing combs in your hair anyway?" he wants to know.

"Where did you find this?" I ask.

"On the floor. Naturally."

We are both cross. Hungry, thirsty, and tired. We glare at each other.

"This comb . . . this is not my comb," I say more to my-self than too him. I have never taken the first comb out of my purse, so now I tuck this one in beside it. Soon I'll have enough combs to open a store.

The guy loves to turn his back on me. I think he is going back to work on the shelf. In a minute he turns around with a mouth full of orange. He is the first one to smile.

"I'm staying on, Emily. I've been promised a roof job this afternoon. You, too, if you want it. But if you want to go back into town now, one of the vans leaves in a few minutes."

I say I'd better go. I didn't leave a note. My parents would begin to worry if I didn't show up this afternoon.

"Thanks for coming with me. I'm glad you decided to. I hope you didn't have a lousy time."

To my surprise I say, "I had a good time." I did! It was fun working with Kyle. And I wouldn't have wanted to miss Ilda.

I find her still in my old dress when I go back through the store to go outside. She is pinning up the hem. She has trouble with the back. I stop to help her. I kneel and pick up a couple of pins. Again she wants to know if I think the dress looks good on her.

"You look like the Queen of the May," I say, which startles her.

"You're making fun of me!" she says, giggling. To my relief she adds, "You're right, this is not a party dress. It's too grand. It's for a wedding. Or I could wear it to church with my black lace shawl. . . . Did you mean it about your party? Am I invited?"

"Absolutely." I mean it this time. Now there'll be two Mexicans there, counting me.

A nagging question floats up in my mind, and I ask, "How did you know who I was?"

"I've heard about you all my life," she says.

I drop a pin. "Heard about me?" Slowly I pick up the pin.

A little uncertainly she says, "My parents knew your mother."

I know immediately she means my Mexican mama.

I bounce to my feet, almost knocking her over.

"Did you know my mama?" I ask.

"No. I mean, I don't remember. I was too young." Ilda blinks two or three times.

"Please, Ilda. Tell me something . . . anything. About my mama . . ." I step toward her, and she backs away.

"Really, Emily, I don't know anything to tell. . . . Let's talk about your party."

I bear down on Ilda.

Mother would be ashamed of me. I am not behaving very well. I can't help myself.

I see something in Ilda's eyes. What is it? Nervousness? Fear?

"You know something! You do! Something about my mama. You heard it from your parents, didn't you? What is it?" I demand.

Ilda is in a crouch in a corner, where I have backed her. She pulls herself up. Her dark eyes half close. She doesn't look very friendly anymore.

"Every Mexican in this town knows every other Mexican. Your mother was Mexican. Of course my parents know her." She pauses, giving me a steady look. "There is nothing strange about it. It would be strange if they didn't know one another."

"Where? How?" I ask.

"They knew your mother married a Petty. Everybody in the county knows who the Pettys are. That's it. And that's all I know. Okay?"

CHAPTER
TEN

I find my mother upstairs in her sitting room working on some papers. She says "Have some" and points to a platter of fruit and crackers and goes on working. I haven't had lunch, so I make a sandwich out of two crackers and a fig.

"What are you doing?" I ask.

"Trying to catch up. Hold it. I'll be through in just a minute." She shuffles through the stack of papers, then puts them aside. Taking off her glasses, she turns to me with a sigh.

"I'm away from the office just one day and . . ." She waves both hands in despair.

"You were going to leave things to other people for a change," I remind her.

She sighs again. "Maybe it's just me. I get nervous doing that. I'm afraid something will go wrong. That's silly, isn't it?"

"Eat, Mother."

We concentrate on the kiwi slices. I make a kiwi sandwich. We start on the grapes. I squash a grape and make a sandwich out of it.

"I enjoyed watching you today," she murmurs. "You looked like you were having such a good time."

"What do you mean?" I ask.

"Like I told you at the clogging demonstration. You seemed to be having more fun than anybody. I didn't know you liked clogging that well."

"It's not my favorite dancing," I say.

Mother gives me an affectionate, forgiving look. "Okay, okay. But you could have fooled me."

I open my mouth to point out I was not at the clogging this morning. I stop. She thinks she saw me there. If I say I wasn't there, I'll have to tell her where I was. Then I'll have to defend myself for going to the barrio without permission. My mouth closes. I chew on a sandwich thoughtfully.

"Mother, I didn't . . ." I begin.

"Oh, yes, you did! Don't deny it! You enjoyed yourself. It makes me feel better about insisting on your clogging lessons. Like I was right after all. In spite of the way you hated it at first."

I didn't hate it. Not really.

I like dance lessons. I love to dance. But when recital time comes and I am onstage, I look out in the audience and find my mother's face. Poor Mother. She wants everything for me. I want to be the best for her. But when I see her smile coming through the dark auditorium up to me on the stage, I almost panic. There is so much hope and fear, both at the same time, in that smile. I can't help but wonder what she is afraid of? That I will fall down? That nobody will like the way I dance? Why does she get in such a fuss?

If I didn't enjoy dancing, I would quit.

On second thought I know I'll never quit. Dancing is part of me. I wouldn't be complete without it. Mother will just have to grin and bear it.

My mother laughs happily. The temptation to keep the barrio a secret wins out. I have never kept anything from her before. I feel a little bad about it, but I feel something else, too. It's as though I am trying out something, something new. Doing something on my own. It is like . . . having an adventure.

"Let's get through, Emily. Your dad's coming home early to take us out to the farm. There's a lot to do.

Mother is referring to Farm Day. My dad is going to open the family farm to the public tomorrow. He does this each year. I am in charge of buggy rides for the little kids. I get all my friends to help me, and it's fun.

She is tapping her mouth with her napkin. Lunch is

over. I had better speak up. I went to the barrio without her permission, but now I have to have it. For something I really want to do. I know she is going to argue. Maybe she will say no.

"Have you heard about the overnight hike?" I ask her. "It's for tomorrow night."

"Isn't it a wonderful idea! New for this year. I wish I were free to go. Why don't you go, Emily? It would do you a world of good. It won't be easy; they are going to hike a long distance, but this is the kind of thing that strengthens a person. Makes you more independent." She is getting up, picking up the fruit tray, and smiling her pretty smile.

"Good idea," I say. Ye gods! What's come over her?

The next morning Kyle calls. He wants me to go back to the barrio with him. I have to remind him about Farm Day.

"I was hoping you could help me with the buggy rides," I say.

"Dad's got me digging a drainage ditch. I'm nowhere near through. That sucker has got to drain the children's playground," he says.

"I'm sorry, Kyle."

"Don't be. I've got a team. It's fun. I mean it. The people bring us bowls of food, hot drinks. It's okay."

I'll miss Kyle's help, but I know I can count on Michelle and Broderick. They worked with me last year and before that, before Michelle was dating, she helped me.

Mother and I drive out to the farm the next day ahead of the crowd and prop the gates open. Dad is on a court case this morning, but he will come out later when he is through. I leave Mother at the old farmhouse and head for the barn where the caretaker, Mr. Mueller, is harnessing the horses. I walk over the pasture beside the barn to look for armadillo holes. There are plenty of them, so I plan the ride route around them.

The people begin to arrive. I keep looking for Michelle and Broderick. It's time to start the rides. I find some kids I know to help me because I can't drive both buggies and Michelle and her guy are nowhere to be seen.

We do the buggy rides all morning. The dust flies; we bump over old corn rows and slosh through a little creek, but the kids love it. By noon I am covered with dust. When I hear the dinner bell, I know the outdoor barbecue is ready and, best of all, I am free to wash up.

I go to the farmhouse again and leave my shoes on the back porch. The house is empty now. Mother is in charge of the barbecue. I strip and get in the tub, a big, old thing standing on lion's feet. It feels wonderful to sink down in water up to my chin. I have had enough of crowds and, for once, I am not very hungry. I decide to stay here awhile.

I go over my conversation with Michelle last night. She was going to come. She couldn't wait, she said, to get behind one of our sweet, old mares and take the kids around the track. What happened to her?

Later, when I am dressed and sitting in the kitchen, my mother comes in. She smells like barbecue sauce. A wonderful aroma. Now I am hungry.

"What have you got?" I ask. She is carrying a covered dish.

"I misssed you. I brought lunch for the two of us. I'll bet you're starved. Why didn't you come to the barbecue?" She stops what she is doing . . . unwrapping the dish. "That's your business, isn't it?" she says, then pulls the dish out of the wrapping.

"I like it here, in the house. Remember, when we used to come out here? When I was little?" I ask.

"We had some good times, didn't we?" She looks around the room. "The rooms are so small! What can you do with rooms this small?" She passes me a plate, and we serve ourselves from the big dish of barbecue.

"Nothing. Don't change this house, Mother. I love it. And its crummy little rooms," I say.

She laughs. "You're absolutely right."

That afternoon takes care of itself. My father has provided for a cane grinding. There will be green cane juice for hundreds of people. Mother and I wander over to the field to watch this event. People of all ages are feeding stalks of cane into the old-fashioned manual grinder, and little kids take turns riding the mule who walks around his endless circle, turning the grinder. When we see Dad's car coming through the gates, we go to meet him.

My father is a popular man. Everybody knows him. Today he wanders through the crowd, stopping to talk every few steps. Mother and I leave him to his public and go back to the quiet of the farmhouse.

About forty minutes later Dad comes to the house. "It warmed up. It's hot out there. Kay, is there any ice in the refrigerator?" He goes to the old icebox and opens the top door. There is a huge chunk of solid ice in it.

"You'll need the ice pick," Mother says. "On the wall, Wesley. It's hanging on the wall, there."

Dad brings his ice water to the kitchen table and sits with us.

I love it. The three of us cramped together in the little kitchen. At this little table our arms touch. We are in one another's faces.

"I love it out here," I say.

"Me, too," Dad says. He looks around. "I was born upstairs. Did I ever tell you that?" he asks me.

"About a million times," I answer. Our blue eyes connect. He smirks, and I smirk back. The three of us listen to the cars leaving. In half an hour everybody will be gone. There will just be the three of us. "You can tell me again if you want to," I tell him.

He looks at Mother. They exchange a pair of smirks. Things are going great.

It is getting so quiet. Country quiet.

"This reminds me of a long time ago," I say. "When we used to come out here. We used to ride together, remember? You'd put me on Old Mary, the grandma mare, and we'd go for rides on the other side of the pasture. Down in the woods."

"You looked so cute on that horse. You could ride at three. I never saw anybody ride like that at that age, did you, Wesley?"

"Oh, Emily is a wonder. To us all. Every day," he murmurs.

I feel sooo good.

"Tell me about me. When I was little. No. When I was a baby," I plead.

My parents sober up. Mother looks at Wesley.

"You want to hear it all again?" Dad asks. "What part?"

"Everything. When Mother married you to get me. And before that. I want to hear about . . . what happened to my first mother. And my twin." This is tough for them, I know. But they nod obediently.

CHAPTER
ELEVEN

"We were living here in this little house when you were born, Emily. After your mother died, I bought the other house, and we moved into town where your grandmother could keep an eye on you," Dad begins.

"No, no, Dad. You're going too fast. Tell about the night of the accident," I say.

My father looks at Kay. I look at her, too. She looks fine to me. Very cool. Comfortable.

"There's nothing new to tell, Emily. Are you sure you want to hear it again?" He pushes his chair back and crosses his legs. "Your mother and Elaine, the other baby, were in the car out for a drive."

"Why did Mama take Elaine and not me?" I ask. I have always wondered, but I have never asked until now.

"You are full of questions tonight, aren't you?" Dad says with a grimace. Again he looks at Mother.

"Didn't your mother have Emily at her house? Baby-sitting her?" Mother asks.

"Probably," Dad concurs. "Probably so."

"I didn't know that. I thought Elaine and I were always together. I thought when one of us went to Grandma's, we both went. I didn't know—"

Dad holds up a hand. "If you don't let me tell this story, we will never get through it before dark."

I realize he is edgy. I know it's hard for him. But how about me? It's hard for me, too. But it's still harder never to hear anything about my natural mama or my twin sister. I miss them. I've missed them all my life. Sometimes I feel like part of me is gone. Like an arm or a leg is missing.

"Your mother took Elaine for a ride. It was getting dark. She came up on the bridge too fast, and the car rolled over the side of the riverbank." Dad stops. There are beads of perspiration on his forehead. He covers Mother's hand with his. They aren't looking at each other. Their eyes are down. Aimed at the tabletop, more or less.

I pick up the story and start telling it myself. "The car tracks were very clear. When the police found the car, they could see clearly where it went over the bank and into the river. But when they pulled the car out of the river, nobody was in it." I pause. "That's the part that's hard for me. Willow River is such a little river. I can't imagine it washing people away forever, never to be found again."

Mother says, "It happened in the spring. After weeks of flooding rains. That river can turn into a torrent. You've seen that yourself, Emily. Remember when I took your Sunday school class tubing down it last spring? Remember how fast it took us?"

"Yes." I think about it. "I guess you're right." Anyway the police thought so. Everybody thought so. Therefore, my mother and my sister were declared dead. Why can't I believe it?

Mother puts her other hand over mine. The three of us are joined by our hands. It is a good feeling.

"Then I lost my mother. She died about two weeks later," Dad says.

Mother squeezes Dad's hand and then mine.

"In a way that's not the end of the story," she says. "Certainly not for me. I moved here just at that time. I found this beautiful child, just a baby really, and her father, both sad and lonely. And I pushed and shoved and fought like a tiger until I got into their lives. It wasn't easy. I had to persist. But look at us! Here we are, a pretty good family. The best, I'd say."

"End of story," Dad says, smiling at her.

"Not quite," I chirp. I feel mean to continue with my questions. But if I have questions, shouldn't I ask them? "Did anybody . . . did you, Dad . . . ever send out, looking for . . . them? Just to be sure?"

Mother gets up and looks in the refrigerator. Dad shifts in his chair and turns so he can watch her. Not looking at me, he says, "Of course." He glances at me, a quick, angry glance. "Did you think I wouldn't?"

"There's nothing in this old icebox, people. We'd better go home and get something to eat. Emily is going on the overnight hike tonight. Did I tell you, Wesley?" She turns around, looking cheerful. "I almost wish I were going. I used to love to camp out. Take a jacket, Emily. The cool weather is coming back tonight."

I am the only kid on this hike. I feel out of place. I didn't know it would be this way. My mother should have come instead of me. There are plenty of people here her age. Why did I come anyway?

There are sixty of us in the middle of the state forest. The hike leaders break us into groups of about twelve each. The camp fire is doused, and we help one another strap our bedrolls onto our backs.

It's too late to back out. We have been hauled out here, into the middle of nowhere, and the Jeeps that brought us are parked for the night at this spot called Campsite One. We have just finished a cookout. It's getting dark fast.

We start, radiating out, every group in a different direction. In just a few minutes, my group is alone. We are on an old logging trail so we can walk in pairs but nobody talks much. The woods close in around us.

When the night falls, some people turn on their miners' headlights. All of us have these flashlight things strapped to our foreheads. I don't turn mine on because I can see the white sandy ruts under my feet even in the dark.

The biggest, reddest moon I ever saw begins to rise in a tangle of tree limbs. There are "Ohs!" and "Ahs!" but I think it is spooky. I shiver. I wish I were back home in my bed.

Someone beside me says, "Are you okay?"

I squint through the dark. All I can see is a shape, a head.

"Sure," I say.

"You are a brave girl. To take this hike. It was designed for seasoned hikers. Did you know that?" the voice asks. A woman's voice.

"No. But I'm strong. I'm sure I can do it," I say, trying to fit her image of me.

What did she say I was? A brave girl?

"I don't doubt you can," she says. "I suppose you'd like it better if there were some young people along."

This is like a question. The kind I don't have to answer if I don't want to.

"I'm okay, really." It is easy to confide in the dark when you can't see anybody's face. So I say, "I did feel funny at first. I thought I'd see a couple of my friends out here. I guess they fell out at the last minute. My boyfriend, Kyle, is so tired every night he goes to bed early, just about this time." I look at my watch. Nine o'clock. "Just exactly this time, in fact. He's been helping out at the barrio. That's our migrant workers' community. Real work. Building. Digging ditches. Things like that. I admire him for it."

"He must be a fine person," she says slowly, as though thinking about it. In a second she asks, "What do you think of the barrio?"

"Me? Oh. I like it. I'm going to get to work on the roofs next time I go. The first time I got stuck working indoors. In the Exchange. That wasn't so bad. There was this girl, Ilda, who works there, too. She's about my age. A Mexican."

She says, like an echo, "A Mexican." She says the word exactly as I did.

We hike in silence for a few comfortable minutes. The moon is climbing up. It is about as high as Venus, the big star that hangs low on cool, clear nights like this. I realize I can see my feet. My legs. I can see the trees on either side of the old trail. I turn to my hiking partner excitedly to say how bright the night is getting.

I see her face!

I can't say a word. She is a Mexican.

She must feel me watching her. She turns her head and looks at me. I can't look away. I feel like . . . she knows what I am thinking. That I am surprised to see her. Again.

"You're shivering, my dear. Do you want my jacket?" she asks.

"No, no, I'm fine," I stammer. I have seen this woman before. I look away, trying to remember where. Then I remember: it was at the Gopher Races. This is Scurvy Dog's mother.

"Haven't I seen you before?" I ask.

She gives her head a little turn to look at me more closely. She is not as tall as I am, and she turns her head a notch more to look up at me. "Some people say they can't tell one of us from another." She laughs. Then she sighs softly.

How could I ever have thought that? Ilda doesn't look like anyone else, and neither does this woman. This woman is the most beautiful person I ever saw. But, more important, she is nice.

She is short and slim. Her hair goes straight back, is held out of her face by two combs, then falls down her back. I realize the reason I didn't recognize her at first. At the Gopher Races she wore her long hair in a braid around her head.

I hope I haven't offended her. I liked the closeness between us. It was so easy, so comfortable. I suppose I was talking too much about myself (Mother says this is rude), but I couldn't help it. This woman listens to everything I say. As though what I say is important. I want her to talk to me some more.

"Uh, have you been a hiker long?" I ask.

"I have always walked a lot." She raises her face to look at the moon. "I like the night."

After that we walk in silence for about ten minutes. I don't hear anything but feet shuffling through sand. Everyone has been murmuring. Now everyone is quiet. There is something about the woods; it listens.

We all give a start as a fox barks in the swamp to the left. A hoarse little yap. This sets off a succession of sounds. Owls call. An awful call. A racket of squawks. A herd of deer are frightened by our approach. They cough as they run. Whispery coughs. Their agile hooves skim the palmettos as they leap off into the night. The last thing we see are their white tails bobbing over the bush.

I feel a hand touch my arm. "Wasn't that a sight!" the woman exclaims in a whisper.

"Deer are good luck," I tell her. "It's good luck to see them."

"Then that explains it," she says.

"What?" I ask.

"My good luck tonight. I am lucky to have you for a hiking partner." She says this lightly. But it makes my heart lift.

Something in this strange woman's voice tells me she means it. She likes me. She is glad I am her partner.

CHAPTER TWELVE

The leaders call a halt. We have walked over twenty miles. We came to the end of the logging trail around midnight and since then have been hacking our way through the bush with machetes. This leaves a trail of our own that the Jeeps will find easy to follow in the morning when they come for us.

It is nearly three A.M. We build a bonfire, and the "cooks" make crackling bread and broth before we spread our bedrolls. The men cluster on one side of the fire and the women on the other. It has turned cold again. I am shivering when I crawl into my bedroll.

I am going to sleep when my new friend, the Mexican woman, whispers to me. I turn my head and look at her. From her bedroll next to mine, she says, "Would you like for me to hear your bedtime prayers?"

My eyes come wide open. It has been years since I said bedtime prayers. I don't want to hurt her feelings. Do I remember a bedtime prayer? All I can think of is, "Now I lay me down to sleep . . ."

I say this childlike prayer into the woman's close, serious face. I feel like I am in a dream. One minute I am saying the prayer and she is listening; the next minute I am asleep. I just close my eyes and am out like a light.

It must be hours later when I come to. What woke me? I am groggy with sleep, but I try to listen, to think. I realize I am cold. Freezing. It is my shoulders. My covering has fallen away from my shoulders. All around my neck someone is tucking the cover in. This is eerie, I think. But instantly I am warm and comfortable again.

Just as I am drifting off I feel one finger brush the hair away from my cheek. I sleep.

When I wake up, the sun is bright in my eyes. More than half the hikers are gone. I sit up and look next to me. The Mexican woman is gone.

Two Jeeps are loading up the stragglers. I jump up and drag my bedding after me. "Let's roll," someone calls, and I crawl into one of the Jeeps. I find out this is the second run. The Jeeps were here an hour ago to take out the first load. What is today? Friday?

I get home to find the house open. Then I hear someone in the TV room. I look in and see my grandfather running old family films.

My grandfather is a busy person. He never seems lonely. But he comes over to run old family movies, usually when we aren't home. He says he does this to "visit" his dead wife, my grandmother. Grandma is on the screen now. And so am I. There I am in diapers reaching up to her. She picks me up.

"Grandpa!" I sit by him and give him a hug.

"What's this in your hair?" He picks pine straw out of my hair. "Where in the world have you been? Somebody's barn?"

The old movie flickers on while I tell him about the hike. Now and then I look at it to see what I am doing up there on the screen. I am into my story about the owls and the deer when I stop abruptly.

"Hey, Grandpa. Can I ask you about my first mama? My parents are burned out on the subject, but I like to talk about her. What did you think of her?"

He turns his face and studies me. Grandpa is old, I know, but he doesn't move like an old man. I mean, he is not decrepit or slow; he is a marathon runner. He lifts weights.

His blue eyes are sharp. Like Dad's and mine.

"I liked her. I've missed her. She was a great woman," he says without smiling.

I can't believe my ears. This is the first time anyone has

ever said something like this. I know Dad loved my mama, but he won't talk about loving her. Just mention her and he gets uneasy. Grandpa seems to like the subject.

"She was?" I ask. I am up on my knees on the couch beside him. Sheer eagerness!

"And pretty. The prettiest woman in our town. When she had you kids, you and your sister, she would parade you around like you were the greatest things since short-bread. Took you with her everywhere she went until she went back to work. She wanted everybody to look at you. Don't take it personally; it was your mama people looked at."

"Went back to work? What did she do?" Why do old people always talk about how a woman looked?

"She was a social worker. A good one, too." Grandpa is slowing down. Having second thoughts, I think. I may have to push him a little to get more out of him.

"Do you think she is still alive?"

"Not a chance, Emily. No way. Put your dreams on something else." He looks back at the screen. My two-year-old self goes off. My three-year-old self comes on. I run to my new mother. She picks me up and kisses me on the top of the head.

I think about what my grandfather said. There is not a chance my mother and my sister are still alive. That is hard to accept, but be honest, I tell myself. He is probably right. Besides, sisters aren't always so great. I have watched other sisters. Some who fight all the time. If my sister had lived, if we had grown up together, would I have liked her? Really, now? There is something nice about being the one and only. For Grandma to pick up. For Mother to kiss. I didn't have to ask for attention from my dad, either.

I look at it the other way. Some kids say I get too much attention. Kyle thinks so. Michelle does, too. They think I am lucky. But always being the center of attention is a pain. Being the only kid, all eyes are on me all the time. It's like I'm in a big spotlight. Everything I do is watched.

If Elaine had lived, there would be two of us. Some-body to take the spotlight off me sometimes. That alone would be worth putting up with the sisterly fights.

There is no way I can be glad my sister is gone. I have wanted her all my life. It's like there is this invisible spot beside me all the time. This empty spot. That Elaine should be in.

I listen. I hear something. A voice. In my head? It says . . . Elaine is not dead. I guess I am hearing what I want to hear.

"When my first mama and my dad married, they lived out at the farm, didn't they? Did she like it out there?" I ask. I am slowing down, too.

"She loved it out there. She loved to ride the horses. And walk the trails. She stayed out there after . . . She didn't want to move into town. Mexicans have a hard time mixing with the rest of us. Some people don't like them." He looks at me again as the film comes to an end. "That's because they don't know them. These small-town people, they're scared of strangers. Strange ways. Strange looks. It's too bad. I think your mama was lonely. I was very fond of her." He gets up. "Got to be going. Time for class."

He is talking about a penology class he is taking at the college. My grandpa is interested in prison reform. He teaches law at the prison in the next county. He was a lawyer like my dad. But never a judge. My dad has taken our family to new heights.

After Dad became a district judge, my grandfather thought I was getting stuck-up. He said, "My mother was a chicken farmer. Fern Petty, for whom this town was named, sold eggs for a living. Sent me to college on her egg money. She had a big mouth. She became a council-woman. Fern Petty, the egg woman, will always be a part of this town's history. So don't forget who you are. Don't forget your roots, young woman! If you'd been born a little earlier, before the chicken farm became a grove, before your dad and I made our money in groves, you'd be gathering eggs instead of taking dance lessons."

What I wanted to say was I am only half a Petty. Only half a Florida Cracker. And I'll never forget the Mexican half, either.

I walk out to his car with him. A neat Mercedes with the top down. He drives off, with the cold air turning his ears red.

I walk around the empty house. Something is going on in my head. But it is a jumble. I can't straighten it out.

Over and over I wish I were back at the old farm. I feel

drawn to go back. To be there. To think. While I am in the shower I make a decision. The farm is only three miles out of town. What's keeping me? That's where I want to be. I'll go. On my bike.

I drop the bike at the locked gate, climb over it, and walk the rest of the way to the house. On the porch are two rocking chairs, but I pass them up. Inside I sit at the little kitchen table where I sat with my parents yesterday. I sit and listen. It is cold inside and out. The house creaks. My hands turn blue, and I rub them together. It is a long time before I get up.

I don't hear voices; I don't see any ghosts, but in an eerie way my feet are drawn to the staircase. I don't decide I'll go upstairs. My feet just take me over to the stairs and up. Am I in a dream?

On the way up the stairs hard winter sunshine comes through a window on the landing. It blinds me for a minute. I rub my eyes. Then I go up the last few steps and am in the hall between the two bedrooms. The nursery on one side, my parents' bedroom on the other. I go into the nursery.

I've been in here a thousand times. The two little beds are still here, still made up with their baby quilts and little pillows. The toy chest is against the wall. I open it. It is not full, but there are still toys in it. Wooden animals. Cloth animals. Dolls. Wagons hitched up to horses. A cornshuck doll holding a baby. A wooden man holding a gun. A hunter, I think. Or an old-timey soldier.

Some of this stuff belonged to my grandparents. And to my dad.

I pick up a doll. A rag doll. I remember her. She belonged to Elaine and me. She was the third sister. There was Elaine, and me and Edith. We fought over Edith.

In all my life I have never remembered about Edith until now. I am crouching in front of the toy chest. I fall back and sit down hard. I am remembering something else. My sister!

Maybe it is just her hands I see. Pulling the doll away from me. I pull back. We are both yelling "Give me, give me!" Then I see this other child. This toddler. I am looking at her, and it is like looking into a mirror. She looks just like me. It is Elaine.

I am cold. When I get up, I go into my parents' bed-room and lie down on the bed. There is an old quilt on it. I pull half of it over me. I guess I fall asleep. When I wake up, I look at my watch. It is just past noon. I get up to go home. My eyes sweep over my parents' bedroom. Quickly I look in the closet. I stand on my toes and run my hand over the top shelf. What am I looking for? I haven't the faintest idea. But I start moving faster.

Now I go through the old chest of drawers. Every one of them. Most are empty. Old sheets are in one. I stand up, thinking: This is silly. Just before I leave the room, I lift the old sheets and look under them.

What's this? Papers.

I sit down on the floor and read. I am reading divorce papers. The divorce of Wesley and Evita Petty. I am frozen with a sudden pain. I don't believe this. I read the papers again. I don't know it when the tears start. My heart, something inside my chest, breaks.

My parents were divorced!

CHAPTER
THIRTEEN

"We were going to tell you on your sixteenth birthday, Emily. That is just two weeks away," my mother says. "You beat us to it by just those two weeks."

I am sitting by myself facing my parents, who sit together on the couch. I am not entirely alone. Edith, the rag doll, is on the floor beside my chair, where I dropped her when I got home from the farm.

Of course, I tore into them. My parents. Accusing. Yelling. Waving the divorce papers. Dad turned six or eight colors and "Forbade me to speak in that tone of voice as long as I live under his roof." But Mother stayed calm.

"I understand how you feel," she says. "You are a big girl now, and you deserve to have the facts. Our only hope is that you will be able to take the facts, to assimilate them. In a mature, realistic way. It was too bad the divorce was followed by . . . the tragedy. But your father didn't cause the tragedy. It sounds silly to have to point this out. It is just there is always the danger of misplacing blame."

"What about the divorce? What about that?" I demand.

"That was between my first wife and me. That was nobody's business but ours," my father says. He is still deeply displeased with me. No doubt about it. He turns to Mother. "This case is adjourned. Permanently. Emily knows now." To me he says, "It's hard to believe now, but this morning I felt very close to you." What is he talking about? This is the first time I have seen him all day. Suddenly he gets up and stands over me. "You are my daughter, and I love you. But you will not ask me questions about my personal life ever again. Understood?"

I don't answer. I don't even look up at him. He marches from the room.

Before Mother can start I say, "It's my personal life, too. Everything that happened to him happened to me."

"Not quite, Emily. Not quite." She doesn't explain. "You are angry with your father right now. But you're overlooking something. You've opened up the most painful part of his life. And you want him to sit still and be pleasant while you ask questions about it. It's like rubbing salt in a wound."

Mother is not as patient as she was. Dad and I are getting to her.

"I think his attitude is lousy." I get up and pick Edith up by an arm. I march out. Just like my father.

"Kyle, it's Emily. Will you go out to the barrio with me?"

"It's four o'clock, Em. Just two hours till supper. What the heck! We can zip out and back if you want to. Your bicycle light works, doesn't it? In case we come back after dark. But why are we doing this?" he wants to know.

"I want to talk to Ilda," I tell him.

I go outside and wait. I am on my bike, pushing off, as he comes along on his. We get almost there and stop at a roadside market. We pool our pennies and buy six or eight bananas. Actually both of us are starving. In between mouthfuls I tell Kyle about the divorce.

"It's tough, Emily. But all this stuff from the past! Isn't it unreal to you?"

"Is a sister real? Is a mother?" I ask.

We are standing beside the market, which is just a shed, dropping banana peels in a crate full of discarded lettuce leaves. I start to cry.

Kyle has just unpeeled a banana. Through my tears I watch him close it back up. He pulls the peelings up, smoothes them, and sets the banana in his bike basket. He puts an arm around me. My nose goes into his chest. I feel his other arm go around me.

He didn't do this very well. He is awkward. He acted like he had to talk himself into every move. But here I am, being comforted.

I cry so long and so hard, he gets used to the situation. If my parents could see me now, they would turn up their heels and die. Cars pass. A car pulls up to the market, and somebody gets out. Two or three people. A family with kids. I sneak a peek at them. The parents are busy pinching tomatoes, but the kids watch me with interest. I look right at one, a little boy, and bawl with my mouth open. He laughs, then looks worried.

Kyle sort of drags me off to one side. "Hey, stop just a minute. I want to ask you something. This may be the time to get it over with."

I snuffle loudly and wipe my nose on his shirt front. He pushes me away from him and holds me by the shoulders.

"This Dean guy, this college kid, is telling everybody you are his girl."

I can see he is asking me a question. "No, I'm not" is all I can say.

Kyle's face is nearly always totally placid. Now it gets tense. His eyes look fierce. "Then, how about . . . why don't you . . . be my girl? Unless you don't want to."

He is something, I think. Something special. I hug him. "I want to," I say. I stop crying and wipe my eyes on his sleeve. He backs away a few inches.

"You do?" His eyes get big. "Then . . . okay!" He gives me a new kind of hug. He holds me close with both arms and puts his lips against my cheek. I move my face around to get our lips together. After a couple of misses we kiss.

I hear a giggle. Kyle and I come apart. I look around and see the little boy, bent over, holding his stomach and pointing. His sister looks. They put their hands over their mouths and laugh.

I feel better. We jump on our bikes, full of bananas and love, and go to the barrio.

Ilda is in the Exchange. She tells Kyle Scurvy Dog is on the new basketball court teaching some little kids to shoot baskets. Kyle leaves us.

Ilda seems glad to see me. If there were any strained feelings between us, they are gone now. I ask her about her new (old) dress.

"Have you worn it yet?"

"I'm saving it for a special occasion," she says. "Don't

you remember? Anyway, I've got another dress for your party."

I am leaning across the counter, and Ilda is sitting on a bench behind it.

"Can I come back there and sit with you?" I ask her.

"Want an orange?" She hands me an orange as I sit down and I start to peel it. "This is like old times." She giggles.

"When I was out here the other day, I was asking you all kinds of things about my mother," I say.

Ilda turns solemn.

"I wasn't very nice about it. But it's hard not to know about your own mother, you know?"

She nods. She sighs.

"Since then, Ilda ... I've found out a lot. The divorce. The whole mess. But nobody will talk to me about it. It's a lonely feeling." I have quit peeling the orange.

Ilda takes the orange away from me and peels it for me. I watch her silently. When she is through, she hands it back to me.

"You must feel awful," she says.

"Awful," I agree. We are both looking down at the orange. She takes it away from me again, breaks it in two and gives me a plug.

"She was a big favorite out here," Ilda murmurs.

"Out here?"

"Why not? She grew up here. Your mother was the only Mexican social worker in the county. My dad says she took care of us. Of all of us Mexican migrant workers. When anybody got in trouble, Evita went to the rescue."

I just look at Ilda. I try not to look surprised. I don't want her to know she is telling me things I don't know. She might stop. But she catches my surprise and explains, "Like when Scurvy Dog got in trouble."

"But he would have been just a baby," I say.

"Oh, no, not the kid." She laughs. "You don't know about that? The guy you do know took his father's nickname. The original Scurvy Dog was his father." I am about to say I know that when she adds, "You ought to know, Emily; it was your father who gave him the name." She is sober again.

"You're kidding!" I say, before I can stop myself.

She studies me.

"I can see why your dad wouldn't tell you that part. He was already married to your mother. She already had the twins, you and your sister, when one of our people got in trouble with the law. Raul. That was his real name. Your dad was the prosecutor in the case. Raul was arrested near the scene of a robbery. There had been a string of robberies. Criminals who took TVs and stuff like that. And took them down to Tampa to sell them."

I want to scream "Go on!" but I wait.

Ilda hands a plug of the orange to me.

"Your mother went to court to be a character witness for Raul while your dad was outside talking to the Tampa press and TV crews. He called Raul a "scurvy dog." The media people loved it. It was so old-fashioned. Your dad talks old-fashioned, doesn't he?"

I say "Yes." I hang my head miserably.

We eat some of the orange. I lift my head. "What happened to Scurvy Dog? I mean Raul. Wasn't he killed?"

"He was killed by a cellmate during the trial. Found dead in his cell one morning. Later he was proved innocent. His son makes everybody call him that awful name. The guy says he will use it all his life in honor of his father. To remind this town what happened." Ilda's cheeks have turned red. Thinking about it does something to her.

We are finishing the orange.

"That's when it happened," she says.

"You mean when my mama divorced my dad?" I ask.

"Yeah. The whole thing started that day. First the divorce. Then the custody battle. My mother says the custody battle nearly killed your mother."

I swallow the wrong way. The last plug of the orange chokes me, and I bend over, coughing. Ilda pounds me on the back.

I stop coughing. I rise up and look hard at Ilda. "You mean . . . are you telling me my parents fought over my sister and me?"

"I thought you knew!" she exclaims.

"Who got us?" I demand. As if I didn't know.

"Your dad."

CHAPTER
FOURTEEN

"I'm sorry, Emily. I didn't mean to give you a shock. But you said you knew everything," Ilda says.

"Then . . . how come my mother had Elaine with her the night they died?"

"She kidnapped her. She went to your dad's house. She had her mother follow her in another car. She sneaked inside. The nursemaid who took care of the children after your grandmother died was bathing you. She had just bathed Elaine and put her in her crib. Your mother picked her up and took her to your grandmother's car. She went back for you, picked you up, and was caught. You were snatched out of her arms. The nursemaid didn't know at that time that the other baby was already outside. Your mother had to leave with Elaine before the police arrived."

"Tell me about the . . . accident," I say.

She hesitates then whispers. "There was no accident. When your mother got to the river, she got out of her car and let it roll over the bank. She got in your grandmother's car. Your grandmother took her and the baby to the airport." She looks over my shoulder and lowers her voice. "Here comes Kyle. That's the end of the story anyway."

Not quite. Not quite. I turn to look at Kyle.

Kyle comes to the counter. "Time to go," he says.

"I'm not going anywhere. Ilda, can I spend the night with you?" I ask.

Ilda looks pleased. "Yeah," she says. "Let me go tell Mama. Watch the store a minute, will you?"

Kyle and I look at each other. He takes my hand across the counter.

"You're not going home tonight?" he asks.

"I don't ever want to see my father again," I say.

He stares at me a minute. "I hate to leave you," he says. I don't answer. "I'll check on you tomorrow." He kisses me.

"Will you watch the store a minute?" I ask. He nods. I go looking for Ilda. I hope her mother won't mind an extra person in the house tonight.

I know where Ilda lives. At least I think I do. But when I start down the narrow, unpaved road that winds through the barrio, I'm not so sure. Especially since the sun has gone down. I can still see; it is twilight; but everyone has gone inside to supper. The barrio has a deserted look.

"Elaine!" someone calls.

I stop. I can feel the hair on my scalp rise.

"Elaine!" the voice calls again.

I look toward a small house on my right. In the doorway I think I see somebody . . . a woman.

The woman comes out on the porch. "Come here, Elaine," she says, looking at me.

As in a dream, I move slowly toward the woman. I take light steps. I feel like I am floating. I get to the porch of the little house and look up.

"Come inside, darling. We must finish our plans. You ran out before I could get through." It is the Mexican woman of the hike. She is the woman I saw at the Gopher Races; she is Scurvy Dog's mother. Or is she?

I follow her indoors. Her small, straight back hurries ahead of me to the little kitchen.

She goes to the stove. I stand in the doorway.

She fills two bowls with food and sits down. I look down at her.

"Come on, honey. Sit down and have your supper," she says.

I sit down to my bowl of beans and rice.

"What's the matter? Don't you like it? Just remember, we can't eat here like we do in California. But this is good, wholesome food. I grew up on it."

* * *

I take up my spoon and put food in my mouth.

"Now, where were we?" She looks at me brightly. "Oh, Elaine! Isn't it exciting? Just think, as soon as you get to the Petty house, I will have your sister here with me. Emily. My own Emily. It will be worth all the hardships, all the risks, to hold her in my arms again." Her dark eyes shine at me. Her beautiful lips part in a smile. Then a worried look crosses her face. "I wish I knew what to say to her. Just how to start. To explain everything. Like watching her at the Gopher Races. How I had to . . . stare at her. I don't want to frighten her. Or give her too much of a shock. I tried to make her feel comfortable with me on the overnight hike. Tell me, honey, do you think we are doing the right thing for Emily? I know it's been a burden for you in a way. But what about her? Will she want to see us?"

"Yes," I say. My whole heart is in the answer. This brings a look of happiness to her face. She laughs out loud with pleasure.

"Okay." She turns businesslike. "You overheard Emily talking to Ilda. Learning all about us. The truth finally. You say she took it pretty well?" She waits for my nod and goes on: "And then Emily said she was going to spend the night here with Ilda?" I nod again. Her voice lowers to a whisper. "I will go next door tonight to Ilda's house. And tell Emily . . . I am her mother. It gives me the shivers just to think about it."

We finish our bowls of beans and rice. She jumps up.

"I forgot the chapatis. I am so excited!" She brings some flat cornmeal cakes out of the oven and puts them on the table. I chew on one.

"Don't eat it here, honey. Take it with you. I can't wait any longer."

She gets up again; she looks at me again. "Do you still want to do it? Are you absolutely certain?"

I look at her blankly. I chew some more.

"I know you are nervous about going into your father's home. If you hadn't thought of it yourself, I don't think I could let you do it." She gazes at me steadily. "Remember, Elaine, every time you get angry with your father, every time you are tempted to blame him . . . or hate him, remember . . . he loves you. He has never stopped trying to find you. If I hadn't changed my name, my whole identity, he would have had you back. The man was hard on me. Not because he didn't love me, but because I left him. He was used to winning. He couldn't accept rejection. Or loss. And it was your loss that caused him the greatest anguish. Try to forgive him. I have."

She hands me a sweater. "If you hurry, you can ride back on Emily's bike with Kyle. He'll think you are Emily, and it will be safer for you to ride with someone else in the dark. Does she have lights on her bike? If not, I'll drive you."

"She has lights," I say.

"Good. Be careful. I love you, darling. Hurry now."

I turn my back and let her help me put on the sweater.

In a low voice she says, "How can I show Emily I love her, too? That I have always loved her, that I have thought of her every day since she was taken away from me? How can I do this, Elaine? I am so nervous. So afraid. What if she doesn't believe me? What if she doesn't want us back in her life? What if I lose her again?"

I turn around and face her.

My heart is pounding so hard I think it will jump out of my chest.

She holds out her arms. I go into them. She is small, but she holds me tightly to her.

"I love you, Mama," I say.

"I know. If I can hear those words from Emily, I will never ask for anything else." We hold each other. She is trembling.

With my head bent down to hers I murmur, "I am Emily."

SECTION II

Elaine

CHAPTER FIFTEEN

Mama and I are moving into our new house. It is a small, neat house in Corte Madera, California, near the top of a hill, with trees on all sides. The road up the hill is narrow with lots of turns. Not a good road. We don't care. For the first time since we moved out here years ago, we own our own home.

"Which room do you want, Elaine?" Mama asks me.

"They've both got big windows," I say.

"I'll take the one on this side, then," she says, and hauls a box into the bedroom at the end of the hall.

I am unloading pots and pans in the kitchen, but I stop and take a look at my new bedroom. I've seen it a dozen times, but now that it is mine, I have to figure out where things will go. First, where will I put my computer? I find the perfect spot. In front of the window. That way I'll have light coming over my shoulder.

The telephone rings. It is Nita, my best friend.

"Yeah. Anytime. Come over now if you want to. You can help me unload," I tell her. I'm glad she's coming over. I want her to see which room I got. And I need to talk to her about something. Mama has a crazy idea. Something she thinks we should do. It worries me.

Nita will listen. When I have somebody to talk to, I can figure out the answers for myself.

"Nita's coming over," I call to Mama.

"Finish your room before you go anywhere. I've got to

go out for something for supper. Lock the door behind me."

I am in the hall, but I run back into my room and watch my mother's car crawl down the hill. Back and forth, back and forth, it takes the turns. It's enough to make you dizzy.

I find the crate with my computer in it and haul it into my room. I have it set up when I hear Nita's little car in the driveway.

Nita's name is really "Juanita." It sounds like a Mexican name, but Nita is not Mexican. One parent is Welsh and the other Jewish. Together with our friends, we could color the rainbow.

Our teachers aren't all one color, either. Two are Orientals, two are black, and four are pink-faced Midwesterners who think their ancesters were Nordic.

Like everybody around us, we feel special.

"I love it," Nita says, gazing out toward the bay. "What a place to work. Or flop around; either one. Lucky you." She flops on the just-made bed.

Nita's family has a lot more than we do. Both our mothers are social workers. But Nita has a father.

I've told everybody my father is dead. Only Nita knows I have a living father who thinks I am dead.

"Want something to eat?" I ask.

"Like what?" She is picking up a small newspaper I have just put down.

"I don't know yet. Mama will be back with food in about ten minutes."

She's looking at the weekly paper my mother subscribes to. It's a small Florida paper from my father's hometown, a place called Fern.

Nita squeals. "Fern? Whoever heard of a town with a name like that?"

"Ridiculous, isn't it?" I agree. I snatch the paper out of her hands. "Listen to this." I read from the paper: JUDGE AND MRS. PETTY HAVE OFFERED TO OPEN THEIR FARM TO THE PUBLIC AGAIN THIS YEAR FOR THE PIONEER FESTIVAL. THE BUGGY RIDES AND THE COOKOUT HELP MAKE THE FESTIVAL A SUCCESS EVERY YEAR. REMEMBER THESE DATES . . . and it gives the dates." I glance over the edge of the paper at Nita. "How about that?"

She grimaces sympathetically. She feels a strand of her

long black hair. After a minute she says, "What is it like to be part of a family like that? Rich. And famous. In their own little county. Do you ever wish you lived there, Elaine? As the daughter of the judge?"

"The truth?" I ask. She nods. "I've wondered about that. Mama and I had such a hard time. You don't know. I can barely remember the worst times. That was when we first came out here. She said we slept on a park bench one night. We couldn't go on welfare. We had no identity. We had to take handouts from people in the Mexican community. We would have starved if we hadn't."

"Don't apologize to me. I'm on your side." She pulls a leg up under her and pounds on a pillow until it suits her, then props herself up on it.

I sit at the foot of the bed. "I'm sure I've told you what we did next? Mama went to work for a vegetable vendor. She had to go to the Farmers' Market at three every morning and buy vegetables and fruit. We were getting to know a few people in the Mexican community where we lived, and usually someone kept me while she was gone. But by the time I was four and five, I went with her. And I worked. Packing tomatoes into crates. Loading cucumbers into the van. Whatever I could do, I did. Which was not much compared with what my mother had to do. Small as she is. But, no. I'd rather have grown up here, just like I did, than with the judge."

"Look out, woman! You are working up to get mad at your old man, again," Nita cautions.

"I live mad at my old man," I say calmly.

"Sometimes you act like you blame all men. Let me say it, Elaine. You just broke up with the first real boyfriend you ever had. A good-looking, interesting woman like you ought to be beating the guys off with a stick. It doesn't make sense: you plus no dates."

"Dating makes me nervous. I hate standing around waiting to be asked for a date. Fact is, I don't have to like any guy if I don't want to," I point out.

For a minute Nita doesn't say anything. She looks at me kindly. Finally she asks me, "Do you want to miss all the dances?" I give her a look. "Okay," she says, "so you don't want to use a guy. You can go alone. But what's wrong with guys? They're people, too. They're just like us. Just as scared. Don't you know that? Besides, you don't have to wait around to be asked for a date. You can ask a guy. . . . It's done all the time."

"I don't know. Every time I see a guy I think I'll like, I wonder if he would do to a woman what my dad did to my mom. You know what I mean?"

"If you make a mistake, if you pick the wrong guy, it's not always fatal, you know. What happened to your mama was bad, I admit it. But that doesn't happen every day."

We are quiet a minute. Nita shifts on her pillows, re-arranges her hair, and falls back. "It's over. It's all in the past. If I were you, I would forget the whole thing. And (as they say on TV) get on with my life."

It sounds good. Maybe I'd be able to do it. Except for one thing.

"Mama and I are going to Fern, Florida, next month," I say.

Now that Nita is in on our plans, we can talk openly about them in her presence. Mama is back from the super-market, and the three of us have taken bowls of fresh blue-berries and a very creamy yogurt out on the deck and are slurping it up.

"I'd be scared out of my gourd," Nita says. "Really, I think you two are the bravest people I know. But are you smart?"

"We are stupid," I say. I follow this with a laugh before Mama can think I am letting her down.

My mother stops eating. She holds her spoon in the air.

"We'll be moved in and settled down here by then. I've already applied for a leave. The time coincides with Elaine's fall break from school. I've got the tickets lined up. Everything is in order. Except a guarantee we will get back here in one piece." Her spoon goes back into the yogurt.

"Can I tell my mom?" Nita asks excitedly.

"I've told Marie already. Only the two of you know."

"Then Mom and I can pray for you together." She smiles, but I know it isn't just a joke.

The dangers are real. Will we be discovered? Will my mama be arrested and put in jail? After all, she broke the law. A serious one. Kidnapping. And the defendant is the judge himself. Does anybody, anywhere ever win a case against His Honor?

Then there is Emily. What I know I don't like. A spoiled brat, if you ask me. Immature. And add to that, her money. She is a country princess. Grew up riding horses. Not stable horses. Her own horses. Her joggers probably cost more than a week's supply of food. Miss Big Frog who lives in a little puddle: the town of her ancestors. Her American ancestors. There is no way we are going to have anything in common.

I say this. But . . . the truth? I have missed Emily all my life. Her I could forgive. My father? That's different. I want to look at him. I want to be hidden in a crowd and study the man. The man who could take my mama's babies away from her. In his court of law. How can Mama say she has forgiven him?

Mama has a picture of him. She brought it along to give to me. She thought I should know what my father looked like. When I look at this picture, all my anger flies out the window. I can't help feeling empty. Pure. Hungry. My father looks like me.

CHAPTER
SIXTEEN

I pull my red hair off my face. I stick my two combs into it to hold it back.

Then for a minute I don't move.

I am standing in a crowd in Fern, Florida. It is Monday, the first day of the Pioneer Festival. I watch my twin sister, Emily.

It is a shock. Here I am standing here. But I am over there, too. Across the street. Another me. I look at her a long time. I don't understand my feelings. I don't think I could like a person of the kind she must be. But the more I look at her the more I want to touch her, to speak to her. I want her to see me, too. I want us to walk up close to each other. And yell. And scream. And laugh. And get to know each other. It is all wrong . . . this being apart all our lives. We should have been together. To fight. To play. I have missed her. I have heard her voice in my dreams.

Just then she turns her face toward me. Now she looks shocked. I turn my face away. I made the promise. I can't walk up to her. Not yet. I start to move away. I look back once. I can't help it. She is still staring at me. I get out of there in a hurry. I walk right into a thick mass of people and move off with them.

We should not have been separated. This thought stays in my mind. I am angry all over again about this. Our father is to blame.

She caught a glimpse of me a minute ago, but she doesn't see me now. I am mostly hidden behind a popcorn machine, peeking around it. I promised Mama I wouldn't let my twin see me. My mother is very nervous about being here. I must help her. Everything must go according to plan.

Emily is with some guy. They are taping the parade. This guy, he looks neat. I've seen guys like him in California. The camera kids. They carry their cameras wherever they go. They all want to shoot real movies. And some of them do. When I am sure Emily is really into float watching, I move across the square to the Petty Building where my father has a suite of offices. I have made a special plan this morning. . . . It doesn't involve my mother. Just me.

Inside the Petty Building I go to the second floor and find the door. On the door it says: DISTRICT JUDGE WESLEY PETTY. I am shaking. Maybe I shouldn't have come.

I didn't promise my mother I wouldn't go to see my father. All I said was I wouldn't reveal who I am to anybody. And I won't. This old guy, my so-to-speak father, is going to think . . . well, let's see what he thinks.

I go inside. I am in a big waiting room. Chinese carpets on the floors. Dark brown paintings on the paneled walls. Huge oil paintings of wide rivers and overhanging trees. And mist and lots of dear, darling nature. All of the paintings look just alike. All are varnished to a hideous orangy color.

"Aren't you going to miss your mother's float?" An old woman is hurrying toward me. She takes my arm and leads me to the window. "Isn't it good! Look at those puppets! It looks like something from Macy's at Christmastime. I know you are proud."

I smile and nod. This woman has me hanging halfway out of the second-floor window of the waiting room. I am afraid she will spot Emily standing right down there on the street below us. Or, worse still, Emily will look up here and see me. Or her "mother" will look up . . . or, good grief! What have I gotten myself into?

"Please, may I see the judge?" I ask, backing away from the window.

The woman turns around and gives me a paralyzed look. Then she giggles.

"Now, that's cute! May you see 'the judge.' Oh, my!" She laughs and looks around. "Did you hear that?" she asks a young man walking by. He is opening a door now. He smiles and disappears.

"Your father—you do mean your father, don't you, Emily?—is in his office watching the parade. What are you waiting for?" She shoos me off.

But I don't know which of six doors leads to my father's office. I look around helplessly. Just then a door opens a crack, and a white head peeks out.

I am struck dumb. That face! That wrinkled, hard-boned little face. Red. No, pink. And those eyes. Diamond bright. As blue as mine.

It has to be my father, doesn't it? But in my terror of making another mistake, I freeze. I smile, just a little smile in his direction to see how he takes it.

"Emily! How nice." He comes through the door. To the woman beside me, he says, "Margaret, when you call out for my lunch, please double the order." Then he comes toward me. "So, you want to watch from up here with me? I am honored." He takes me by the arm and leads me into his office.

My legs are weak. I fall into a chair. The chair is so plush, I sink up to my waist in it. I am nervous but excited. So far so good. But what now?

My father has gone to a huge wide-open window. The heavy drapery is pulled to one side. From here all I see behind him is sky.

He turns. "Where are you? Come over here."

I stand beside him, and he puts an arm across my shoulders. He has to reach up to do it. I am taller than the guy. I bend down to make it easier. I sneak a look at him. That face is aimed down at the street parade. Smiling. Pleased. He turns to look at me. He looks like he likes what he sees.

"This is great! I didn't expect you. Surprise me more often, will you?" He is close to me. Gazing fondly at me. I try to look back at him in the same way, but I can feel my face stiffen.

Our eyes are in some kind of locked position. His smile begins to fade, and he looks alert.

"Is something the matter, my dear? You did come up here to watch the parade with me, didn't you? Or is it something else? Do you want to tell me something?"

"Uh, no," I say airily. But my voice breaks.

"Well, so!" He has stopped watching the parade. This guy is sharp. He is watching me like a hawk. I must be careful. In a minute he says, "Both of your mother's floats have gone by. Maybe you'd rather sit down and talk?"

I nod and move with him back to my chair. It swallows me again. He sits on his desk. On that huge desk. He looks like a sailor, just a speck of a person, on the wide deck of a ship.

"Is it about your mother, Emily?" he asks, bending toward me.

"No, uh, yeah, maybe so," I mutter.

The alert look comes on again. "You can tell me. Speak up," he says.

I try to give this some thought. But I don't have time. I blurt out, "You know how she is! I don't always know how to handle the situation." Every kid says this about her mother at some point. I hope it sounds like a routine complaint.

"Ah!" He sits back and sighs deeply. The hard reddish hands come out and clutch a knee. He is rocking back on his little butt with one knee in the air. Worriedly looking at the ceiling.

"You're almost sixteen, Emily. You will understand what I am going to say." He rocks some more. Then he swings forward the stops. "Granted, she is overprotective. She is so wrapped up in you. Always has been. In her case it is natural to be a little watchful. And possessive. I've seen this happen several times. A woman who can't have a baby—I am talking to you, man to man—gets a baby, somebody else's baby, adopts it, and Voilà!—it becomes her prize possession."

"Your wife . . . uh, my mother, couldn't have a baby?" I ask, curious.

"I am telling you this in confidence. This is just between us, understand? Kay might not like it. That we talked about her. But I want to give you some background. So you won't be so hard on her."

"What about you?" I ask.

The blue eyes stare at me. "Me? Me what?" he asks.

"Are you overprotective, too?"

"Of course not. Good heavens, no! You will soon be on

your own. In college in just one more year. I can handle it." The man looks irked with me. What did I do?

"Haven't I always said you should be allowed to live on campus. You can spend the weekends at home, but I've always been willing for you to move over to the campus when you start your freshman year."

"What campus?" I want to know.

He laughs. "The only one in town. Unless you know of another one."

"Suppose I don't want to go to the local college?" I ask.

He turns loose of his knee and sits up, very straight. "Why wouldn't you want to? Has somebody talked you out of it?"

This makes me mad. Why does he assume somebody can talk me out of something I want to do. Doesn't he know I can think for myself?

I give him a look he won't forget. "Just a minute..." —I stop and add "sir." I remind myself to keep my voice cool. "Are we talking about where you will go to college? Or where I will?"

His whole face looks blown out of shape. He comes back with a dazed expression.

I try to soften my voice a little. "Because if we're talking about me, I'm not going to any local college. It isn't just four years I want. Or a diploma. What I want is a school that will help me, *me*, as in my special interests." I stop before I tell him my special interest is computer science. I don't know how Emily feels about the subject. But I must have made my point. His face is coming back together. I add, "I am looking the whole country over. This is work. Lots of letter writing. And it's important for me to find the right place." Another thing I don't tell him is I have already narrowed my choices down to three universities.

"I didn't realize... you had thought about it in this way." He takes a deep breath. "I admire your determination." In another second he smiles, a dried-up little smile.

I didn't mean to ruin his day.

Our eyes connect. He drops a hand over mine. This does something to me. I look down at our hands and then back at my father.

What happened to hating him? His touch . . . it is gentle. But I still don't like him.

"You are a Petty, Emily. A Petty through and through. Will you think me boastful if I say . . . I didn't realize how much alike we are? You and me?"

He takes my hand and holds it in both of his. I can't hate him. I can't. I've been with him fifteen minutes in twelve years and already I can't hate him.

"My dear girl! I am proud of you . . . all over again. Now, let's have—"

There is a knock at the door.

"Our lunch is here. Can you stand hot crab salad again?" he wants to know as he goes to the door.

I am so hungry I could eat the claws off a buzzard.

CHAPTER
SEVENTEEN

I have a million different feelings when I leave my father's office. The idea I came here with—that he was hateful—won't work anymore. He is a little stiff, but he can be kind. He can be understanding.

I am walking fast. I've got to get back to the barrio where Mama and I are staying. I don't want to mess up my mother's plans. I mustn't be recognized as the "other" twin.

Someone comes up behind me.

"Hey, you dropped your comb."

Is this the oldest trick or what? Before I look at the guy I feel my hair. Okay, the comb is gone. I look at the guy.

He is a blond guy. If I were interested in "gorgeous"—but I'm not.

He holds the comb out to me. "This is yours, isn't it?" He talks like a Southerner. Not just a Floridian. Deep South.

I accept it. His expression is . . . nice. I can't help but smile. We have both come to a stop. As I pull my hair back and tuck the comb back into place, I say, "How did you know?"

"The first time I saw you you were wearing the combs. The next time I saw you, you weren't. You were with some guy who was taping the parade. When I found the comb, you were gone." He speaks slowly. He is doing a slow scan of my face. He seems to be enjoying himself. His eyes do a job on my nose. Then my cheeks. Now down to my neck. Back up. I have the feeling he thinks I would taste good.

"What are you? Some kind of detective?" I ask. I fling this at him, but I am still smiling. I like his face! I want to say he has a sweet face, but that's ridiculous. This guy is man-size. He's got a lean nose. He's got gray-brown eyes, the color of dark toast. No, that's too dark—the color of mushrooms in butter.

He dips his head as though in thought. "I hadn't thought of myself as a detective. I'm just a guy who wants to know your name. But I don't want to be rude."

He is sweet! I know my smile is spreading all over my face. From my mother I got this great big mouth, and I can split my face wide open from ear to ear. It's not a pretty sight, so I try to keep it under control. But right now, looking into this sweet face, my smile goes way out of bounds.

"I'm glad you smiled. I was beginning to think you didn't like me," he says.

"I like you." That's what my mouth opened and said. Straight from my heart.

He ducks his head again and says, "I'm Dean Hampton. I'm new here. This is my first year at the college."

I start to say I am new here, too. What a dumb thing to say! As long as I am here in Fern, Florida, I have to pass for my twin. I remember this just in time.

"I am Emily Petty. I've lived here all my life."

He looks surprised. "You don't talk like a Floridian. Not at all. I'd have guessed you were from the West. Where people talk like newscasters." He jerks his head up and puts out a hand. "I don't mean that like it sounds! I wish I could talk like that. I want to go northeast to graduate school someday. I don't want to sound like a hayseed when I get there."

"You don't. I love the way you talk." We aren't saying anything. Nothing important. But something very important is happening. I can feel it. When we stop talking, we look at each other. Just look and look. I don't think I will ever get enough of this guy's face. The way he looks at me . . . it makes me wonder if he feels the same way.

We are walking, slowly, very slowly, toward the popcorn machine. We pool our pennies and buy a bag of popcorn. We sit on a bench and eat some of it. I keep a sharp eye out for any member of the Petty family. None of them shows up.

"What was it like growing up here?" he asks.

"It must have been awful! I mean, it could have been awful, but I guess I like it all right." I am wondering if this is what Emily would say.

"You have a beautiful home. The big trees and the way your family keeps the grounds . . . reminds me of my home-town, Charleston, South Carolina."

I get a quick, cold dart of fear. Can I carry this off? What have I gotten myself into?

"You've seen my house?" I ask cautiously. I haven't seen it myself yet.

"This morning before the parade I took the bus tour. It doesn't go very far. It takes only about half an hour. There isn't much to see here in Fern. Except for your house." He laughs. "The tour bus driver kept driving back by it every few minutes. He took us to see the old cemetery. Then he took us past your house. 'The pride of Fern,' he called it. Next he took us to see the park by the river. He called the river 'Tragedy Creek.' Said some woman and her baby were drowned there. Then back by your house again. Next we went to see the Episcopal church. The oldest church in the county. And then, you guessed it, back by your house." He is glancing at me every now and then. When he finishes talking, he gets this odd expression. "How dumb of me! I've embarrassed you! I ought to have my head examined." He turns pink around the ears.

I know the guy hasn't done anything wrong. But I am getting very uncomfortable. First, I don't like having to pretend to him I am my sister. Second, I hate it that he thinks I live in her house. And third (and this is the worst), I hate it that he likes her big, old house. Maybe this is all he likes. He knew all about this Emily person before we started talking. Maybe he wanted to meet . . . not me . . . but her. The girl with the big house. The girl who passes for a Scotch-American. The girl nobody knows is Mexican.

Why do I ever fall for a guy?

"Thanks for finding my comb. I've got to go." I get up and start off, walking fast.

The guy comes after me. Runs after me. "Wait. Please." He is walking beside me. "Emily, please."

I stop and look at him. There goes my heart again. I can hear it thumping. Am I falling in love?

"Let me make up for . . . whatever I did to make you mad. Where are you going? Let me give you a lift. Please."

I stick my nose in the air and say, "I am going to the barrio. To do some good deeds. For the poor Mexican migrants. Want to go slumming with me? Of course, I can't ask you in. But you can drop me off if you want to."

That's how I get home. Dean drives me to the barrio.

"I'm going to look for you tomorrow," he calls after me.

"I don't think I can get away," I say, and leave him sitting in his car before he can ask for an explanation.

CHAPTER
EIGHTEEN

It is Tuesday morning, the second day of the Pioneer Festival. I am staying here at the barrio today. My mother is getting ready to go to the Gopher Races. The Gopher Races? Did I hear that right? Mama says, "Yes, and don't be so snooty."

Oh, my! I cover up my head and try to go back to sleep.

We are staying in a little house with Ilda on one side of us and a guy named Scurvy Dog on the other. I know all about him, but I haven't seen him yet. Mama says Scurvy has caught a tortoise and is going to enter him in the race. Too bad I can't go with her to watch. But my twin will probably be there. I mustn't be seen where Emily is. That would upset my mother's plans for the three of us.

"I am a little nervous," Mama says, standing in the doorway of our bedroom. I sleep on one side of the room on a cot, and Mama sleeps on the other side in a bed. It's not very comfortable. I watch her braid her hair and wind the braid around her head. As always, she looks good. I used to wish I looked more like her, but to do that, I'd have to give up my red hair. My red hair is my favorite feature about me. It makes people stare at me, and I am a hog for attention.

"Don't be nervous, Mama," I say, yawning.

"I can't help it. This is the first time I will see my other child . . . in more than twelve years." Her voice shakes a little. "This means so much to me. . . ."

What can I say? I sit up and swing my legs over the side of my bed.

"I'll pray for you," I tell her. I add, "For Emily, too."

She looks at me thoughtfully. "Are you feeling better toward Emily?" she asks. I nod. Mama takes a breath. She says, "How do I look?"

"She's not going to see you, is she?" I ask.

"I can't keep her from seeing me. But she won't know who I am. Do I look all right?"

"You are so pretty, Mama, that even my girlfriends are jealous of you," I say.

She beams.

"I better go now on the strength of that. I'm sorry you can't go, too. We'll try to get you out tomorrow." She walks to my bed, bends over and kisses me on the head.

After Mama goes I dress and find Ilda in the Exchange. We unpack new stock. Old clothes, old shoes, old pots and pans. It is all new to the migrant community.

Ilda and I get along really well.

"Who is your boyfriend, Elaine?" she asks.

That's always one of the first questions girls ask when they meet you. It makes me sick.

"I don't have one," I say.

"I thought you got a ride home with that blond guy yesterday afternoon. From my window he looked great. Don't you like him?" she asks.

"No. Actually yes. Oh, I don't know. Let's talk about your boyfriend."

"I haven't got one, either," she says. "I like Scurvy, but I hate his name. And it's not just his name that bothers me: it's the way he hangs onto it."

"I agree. What is his real name?"

"Raul. A good name. His father's real name. That's what I call him, but he won't answer to it. He is one stubborn kid." Her dark eyes roll.

"When do I get to meet him?" I ask.

Ilda and I are about to close the Exchange for the noon hour when Scurvy Dog comes through the door.

"I thought I left you with Kyle," he says.

He thinks I am Emily. I am about to tell him who I am when he says, "Or did you go off with the blond guy?" He laughs in a teasing way. "Just teasing," he says. "I don't think Kyle knew what was going on. You vamp. You flirt. You charming wench."

That Mexican guy is the best-looking person I have ever seen. But I am in love with somebody else. And I have just learned my twin was with the guy I love. Today.

Ilda quietly steps between us. "Can you keep a secret, Raul? This is not Emily. This is her twin, Elaine."

The guy is really knocked back. After the first real surprise, he pretends to be shocked. He staggers backward. We laugh at him.

"Now I see what they mean by identical twins. How do you tell yourselves apart?" he asks.

"We have never met," I say. "We've been separated. . . . You know the story. I'm the one who drowned in the river."

That slows him down.

"That's right. I remember that part of the story. Welcome back," he says. "Let's celebrate. Let me buy you an orange juice." He leads me back to the bench behind the counter while Ilda locks the door. When she sits down beside me, he hands us our juice.

"To the risen dead," Scurvy says. We tilt our bottles up and drink. He is through first. "So you don't know your sister yet? I like Emily. But not her dad. Her old man is trying to change his image. From mean to nice guy. I don't buy it. He is too rich for my blood. Kyle says he's going to give Emily a car for her sixteenth birthday. Anything else you want to know?"

"Is this Kyle . . . is he Emily's boyfriend? Or is the blond guy her boyfriend?" I ask.

"I don't know. Is it important? Okay, then. I'll find out tonight and let you know." He turns to Ilda. "Ilda, I've been invited to Michelle Mackenzie's house tonight for a pizza party. Want to come? Michelle said I could bring a girl."

"I can't. I'm baby-sitting tonight," she says.

"I'll bet you wouldn't come anyway. I'll bet you'd be too chicken to go to a party in town," he says.

"I'm not afraid. But I might feel funny. The town kids never do invite us to anything. How come you got invited?" she asks.

"It's my fatal charm," he says. "You may not appreciate it, but . . ." The two gaze at each other, and I feel like I'm peeking in at a private scene. I clear my throat. I say, "Raul. Can I ask another favor?" The guy remembers me and turns around.

"I want to get out of here tomorrow. I can't go up to town if Emily does, you see. Do you think you could get her out of the way? Take her for a stroll in the country? So I can get to the Clogging Demonstration? I love clogging. And I think I'll go nuts if I have to spend another day unpacking boxes of old clothes."

"I couldn't get Emily to do anything. I don't know her that well. But Kyle is coming out here tomorrow with his dad." He thinks while he talks. "I could say 'Why don't you bring Emily with you?' "

Ilda and I are alone in the Exchange through the lunch hour. We make ourselves a couple of sandwiches. I get restless.

"Ilda, how about if we catch a bus and go uptown? Maybe see the tennis tournament? There'll be a crowd. We can get lost in a crowd," I say.

I am thinking Dean may be there. But! But what if Emily is there, too?

I say, "Maybe we shouldn't. Emily may be there."

Ilda studies me. "I could stick your hair up in a hat. Let's see what we've got around here."

With a spurt of new energy we both ransack the place looking for suitable hats. We try on several. All of them are awful. Ilda goes into the stockroom and brings out still another box. The label says: HATS. We open it.

It is bulging with giveaway baseball caps. I put one on. Just above the bill of the cap is the name of a bank in town. Ilda stuffs my hair up inside the cap. It won't all go inside. She pulls some hair through an opening in the back of the cap. A ponytail. I decide I look neat.

Ilda wants to wear one of the caps, too. We get her hair in it with a tail coming out of the back. We look in a mirror. With our hair pulled away from our faces we don't look so different anymore. Big cheekbones. Big mouths. We laugh and point at each other.

Ilda gets a friend to watch the store, and we catch a bus

for town. The bus takes us to the square and starts to circle it.

I am looking down from my bus window on the passing cars. The traffic thickens. The bus begins to crawl. Then it comes to a complete stop. We are in a traffic jam.

A station wagon creeps up beside the bus. It is wedged in between two other cars. I am looking at the driver of the wagon. An older man. Sitting beside him is a beautiful black woman. She is in long Victorian tennis whites. I am hoping she is going to win her game today.

My eyes move back to the window behind the driver. There is a face. My face. It's my twin!

My heart contracts. She is staring at me. She looks . . . what? . . . frightened? Like she's seen a ghost. That's it. She thinks I'm dead. But she can't know it's me. My hair doesn't show. I remember my ponytail. I think I should back away from the window, but I can't move. Something terribly intense passes between us. I want to tell her it's me. I want to say "I am Elaine; I am your sister." Something tells me she knows me. And hears me thinking.

I press my nose to the glass and whisper "Emily!"

The station wagon moves forward. The bus moves, too. We go past each other and out of sight. When I can't see my sister anymore, I wonder at my feelings. I am really mad at her for trying to take Dean away from me. And I am disgusted with her life-style. But when I look into her eyes . . . I love her. She stays in the middle of my heart all through the game.

I watch the tennis tournament without worrying about *detection*. After all, *Emily* was riding in the opposite direction, so I know she won't be there. I like watching the black woman. She wins her game just as I had thought she would.

But Dean doesn't show up.

Ilda and I catch another city bus and go back to the barrio.

Except for my glimpse of my twin, the trip uptown is wasted. A dry run. I've got to make a plan. I've got to think of a way to see Dean again.

* * *

Mama is home when I get there. I start to tell her about seeing Emily when she grabs me and gives me a hug. Holding me, squeezing me in half, she says, "I saw her, Elaine! I saw her!"

I sort of dance her over to a chair and sit her down. I stand in front of her. She shines. She shines all over. She is breathing in big gulps.

"You saw Emily?" Silly question.

"She is not quite you. She is different." She ripples the air with her fingers. "She is not an old-fashioned Southern belle, nothing like that, but she is . . . quieter than you. No, that's not the word. Maybe she doesn't have your confidence, I don't know, but she hangs back just a little. She is so . . . dear! Not childlike. Not immature. But . . . you know what it is?"

I say "What?"

"She needs her mother." She announces this for a fact.

"But you said you found out she had a good mother," I protest.

"She does. I don't know how to explain what I saw. Or felt. Maybe the feeling was just my imagination. Maybe I want her to need me."

We are on dangerous ground here. I think about it. "Maybe. But maybe you saw something else about her. Maybe our little rich girl is a poor little rich girl who needs something she hasn't got. Even though she seems to have everything." Except my mother. Her mother.

Mama's shine fades. She folds her hands in her lap in a way she has of doing when she wants to calm down.

"You and I have always helped each other. Elaine, my Elaine. What would I have done without you? I love you, and nothing will ever change that," she says.

I feel ashamed. Of being jealous of Emily. Where my mother is concerned, there will be no cause. "I am going to help you with this, too. We three, you, my sister, and I, are all going to be together. You'll see." Where Dean is concerned, I am still jealous of Emily. But for my mother I will keep it under control.

"That is what I need to hear," she says. She is about to get up when I sit on the floor at her feet.

"Go on; talk about her. I know you want to. And I want

to hear everything. What did she do? Did she see you?" I ask.

Mama brightens. She sits forward on the edge of the chair. "Once. I think she looked right at me once. But this young man came up to her, a young blond man, and they walked off together. Her date, I guess. He was very handsome. They looked beautiful together. You should have seen them. . . ."

I get up. "I'm hungry, Mama. Can you tell me the rest while we fix supper?" I don't want to hear. It goes all over me that my twin was with Dean today. Just because I couldn't be there. It's me he likes.

Or is it me? Maybe it's Emily he likes.

Something tells me my jealousy just got out of control.

I've got to do something. I've got to get out of here. Get with Dean again. If only Emily *can* be got out of the way. If only Scurvy can get Kyle to bring Emily out here tomorrow. If only I can sneak past them and go to the Clogging Demonstration. I have a feeling Dean will be there looking for me.

There are a lot of "if onlys."

CHAPTER NINETEEN

The next morning, Wednesday, I am dressed and hanging around the Exchange. It has warmed up. Too warm for a sweater. Ilda and I keep looking out the window to see if Emily is going to arrive.

"I can't wait to meet this Emily," says Ilda. "I know her. I see her at school almost every day. But she doesn't know me. I can't believe I am going to spend the morning with the town's number-one debutante."

I listen to her with a small smile. Part of me likes to hear about what a snob Emily is. Part of me wants to defend her.

"Maybe she's not so bad," I say.

"Maybe. But Raul had a lousy time at Michelle's party last night. That's Emily's crowd. I can't help it, Elaine; I resent them. What makes them so special? They're no smarter—most of them aren't as smart as Raul, or as good-looking."

"I know. Don't worry about them. Just remember who you are. Mexicans are the proudest people in the world. We know more about our ancestors than they know about theirs," I tell her. It may be true, but I know it is not much consolation. You can't stand on your ancestors' shoulders.

"Who is that getting out of the van?" Ilda peers out of a window. "Oh, I know him. That's Kyle." She looks around at me. "Get out of here. There's a redhead right behind him. It must be your sister."

I get one quick glance. It is Emily. It is hard to look

away. To leave. I've got to go into the dark stockroom. I hide among some barrels of beans. I hear the Exchange door open, and then the place fills with voices.

The Exchange must have two-dozen people in it, I think. All those footsteps! The voices grow louder. They burst into the stockroom. I scrunch down lower. I am on the floor now, bent over, between the bean barrels.

A light comes on, and some guy begins to "assign jobs," whatever that means. I rise up just a little and peek between the barrels. I watch kids troop outside in bunches. Soon nobody is left in the stockroom except the older guy and two kids. One has red hair! The other must be this guy, Kyle.

The three of them decide Kyle and Emily will work in the stockroom.

I almost die. Have I got to stay scrunched up behind these barrels in this dark corner all morning? Thank goodness it's warm. The stockroom was chilly yesterday.

They start to work. An inventory! They'll never get through. My day is ruined.

I can't see them much. Just now and then. Just a glimpse of skirt or leg.

I slump down. I get in a more comfortable position and prepare to sweat it out. It takes about an hour. I'm sore all over. Finally Emily goes into the Exchange in the front of the building.

I wonder if I should make a dash for it. I know Ilda will try to keep Emily in the Exchange to give me a chance. I decide to try it. I come out from around the barrels from the direction of the Exchange. I walk right up to Kyle and say, "Be back in a minute." I start for the back door.

"Hey, Em. I thought you were going to bring me a snack. Where are you going now? Stick around. I like your company, snack or no snack."

I step outside. I hear him calling after me, "You dropped your comb."

He can have it, I think; I'm on my way.

I hurry to the corner and catch the bus uptown.

I am looking everywhere for Dean. I wander through the crowd gathering beside the bandstand in the courtyard.

The cloggers are streaming across the square in their red-and-white costumes.

How am I going to clog without a costume? Where is Dean?

Maybe Dean won't be here today. My heart sinks.

Someone comes up beside me, smiling. A tall woman with wide, pretty gray eyes. She scowls and smiles at the same time.

"Hurry, darling! It's almost ten-thirty. I was afraid you were going to be late." She gives me a big kiss on the forehead and scowls some more. I know I am "Emily," but who is she? "I don't remember that shirt. I didn't know you had a red shirt," she says.

She hurries me into the courthouse, where other girls my age are changing into their clogging togs in a dressing room.

"I found my daughter," the tall woman calls out to another woman. "Did you find yours?" she asks.

The woman answers yes, they both laugh, and then my "mother" turns her attention on me.

I have the costume on. It is a perfect fit. My "mother" fastens the zipper in back, turns me around as though I am a wooden doll, and stands back to look at me.

"You look beautiful. Just beautiful." She scowls and smiles some more. All at once she is all scowls. "What in the world did you do to your hair?"

I reach for my hair, wondering. "It may need combing," I say. I pull a comb out of the side of my hair and comb my hair back with it. Then I do the same thing with the other comb and the other half of my hair. I look at the woman to see if she approves. She looks horrified.

"Where did you get those combs?"

I am surprised. Maybe astounded. Does Emily have to answer questions like that?

Before I can say anything she says, "Oh, never mind about the combs. If you like them, they'll have to stay. But the color, Emily! I thought you loved the color we got with the toner." Now she looks hurt.

"I put toner in my hair?" I ask, astonished. I catch that one as quickly as I can. "I washed it out this morning. How do you like it?" Her face is having some kind of private battle with itself. Her mouth opens and wiggles but doesn't say anything. I decide to help her out. "I love the color of my hair . . . Mama. Why hide it?"

"Since when? You have complained all your life about your hair. It attracts attention. Everybody stares at you. It's the color of rotten oranges. Mashed-up carrots. I don't know what all!" Again the woman stops, and her face goes back to its silent battle. Now the eyebrows shoot up, and the nose twitches. "On the other hand," she begins grimly, "I shouldn't fuss because you have decided you like it, now, should I? And if you want to call me 'mama,' that's all right, too."

Oops! I think. I say, "I'm glad you don't want to fuss. Because we don't have time. Not if I am going to get up on that stage before the clogging begins." I look up at the wall clock.

The dressing room is empty except for us. My "mother" grabs me by an arm, and we go outside.

"Please, Mama," I say gently. "I can get on the stage by myself."

She turns me loose like my arm is made of sizzling metal. I start to climb the steps to the stage. She gives me a strange, wild smile. Impulsively I bend down and kiss her on the forehead.

The big eyes light up. She smiles, and her large, even white teeth bask in the sunlight. We wiggle our fingers at each other, and I prance onto the stage.

Several girls speak to me. One girl, a real beauty everybody calls Michelle, gets beside me.

"Did you see him?" she asks in a whisper.

"Who?" I whisper back.

She looks at me like I'm crazy "Your new guy, of course. Dean."

"Where?" I demand.

She points. I look. There he is. Looking back at me. Not smiling. I smile and wave. He doesn't raise a hand. I turn to Michelle as the music starts.

"What's the matter with him?" I ask.

"After the way you treated him at the Gopher Races? What do you expect? I can't believe you'd take Kyle over this guy."

The music begins, and we start to dance. At first I give it an easy, very light slap with my foot. Then the other. I tilt my body. I swing up a leg and put my hands on my hips. I know I look good. I've got a great body. And this costume fits me well. Maybe it is a silly costume; all clogging costumes are a little bit silly. The dance step can be silly, too, unless you throw yourself into it.

I look at Dean again. He looks away, but not before I catch him watching me. I wish he knew it wasn't I who made him mad. What can I do? I swing my hair and lift a foot again; then I come down with a stomp that shakes the stage.

That gets his attention. I want to say to him he was wrong about me. I'm not this country princess who lives in the biggest house in town. I am Elaine. There is nobody like me, not even my twin. I lift a foot, bring it down, and shake the stage again.

The rest of the dance is pure joy. I am into it. I forget everything, even my gorgeous guy. My body lifts and turns and spins and sweeps around the stage, stomping all the way. Once I bring my arms up in a little bit of Mexican side effects just for the fun of it. I dance this way for a full moment. Arms up, body lifting and swaying, feet coming down like gunfire. Somebody claps. Others start clapping.

I find myself dancing alone, down center stage. The other cloggers have backed off behind me. I go for it, adding a few totally uncloglike pirouettes just for the heck of it. When I finish this impromptu solo, I come forward and give a big arms-out curtsy, bend my head, and flop my long red hair over so it trails on the floor. The applause lasts and lasts.

Sweat runs down my neck and across my face. But I feel great.

I prance off the stage beside Michelle, who gives me a wide-eyed look. My "mother" waits for me. Right there in front of everybody, she holds out her arms. Am I supposed to run into them? I grab her hands and peck her on the cheek, looking around for Dean.

I spot him. He is coming toward me. Not too fast, not too eagerly.

"Excuse me," I say to "Mother" and Michelle. "I'll be back in a few minutes." I walk away with Dean.

* * *

We find a tent vendor selling frozen yogurt, and Dean buys yogurt cones for us. We lick our cones under an oak tree away from the crowd.

"May I ask what's going on, Emily? One day you like me, the next day you don't. Today . . . do you?" he asks.

"I do. I do," I say.

He melts. A hand comes up and holds onto my arm. "Let's keep it this way." The hand slides down and takes my free hand.

Suddenly the frozen yogurt tastes delicious.

"When can I see you?" he wants to know.

Now what? I hesitate. I make a thing of finishing my cone and throwing it in a trash bin. He tosses his in after mine. I can't think what to say. He answers for me.

"Tomorrow would be a bad day, wouldn't it? I mean, your whole family has to stay at the farm all day tomorrow. You are in charge of the buggy rides for the little kids, aren't you? I could come out, but I might be in the way," he says.

"Don't do that! I mean, yes, you'd be in the way," I tell him. Immediately I am sorry. He looks, not mad, but hurt.

"I don't mean that, Dean. You could never be in my way. I want to be with you. Anytime. It's just that . . ." I come to a stop. Again I don't know what to say.

"Emily. Tell me what it is. I'll do anything to please you if I know what you want. He turns me toward him. "We are having some sort of trouble, and I don't know what it is. Every time your left eyebrow wiggles, you give me a hard time. See, it's wiggling, so I know you aren't leveling with me. Give me a break. I think about you all the time. I like you more and more. I can't say what I want to say here in a public place. Can't we get together sometime, somewhere?"

I want to be with him, too. Somewhere. Soon. I touch my left eyebrow. I smooth it out. I think: he sees through me, and he is hurt.

My mind races. It hops on an idea. I blurt out, "Come to see me tomorrow. At my big house. No, I won't go to the farm. I'll stay home and wait for you."

He smiles, takes both my hands, and sways toward me. "All right! What time?"

"Early. Say, ten o'clock? Bring your bathing suit. I hate

to stay inside." I know I am sounding idiotic. "With this change in the weather I thought we might have a swim and hang around the pool."

"A girl with a pool! I like that." He seems to be joking. But who knows?

Tomorrow morning I'll find out if it is me he likes. Or if it is Emily and her swimming pool.

CHAPTER
TWENTY

"Here comes your mother. I've got to go anyway." He squeezes my hand, nods at my approaching "mother," and whispers, "See you tomorrow."

"You were just . . . wonderful! I never saw you dance any better, Emily. Everybody is talking about it," she says. She tries to do the old arm-grab trick, but I avoid her. I wonder where she wants to pull me off to now?

"Time to go home, darling. We'll have a late lunch together, just the two of us."

"Why don't we get a snack here . . . Mother?" I say. I can slip away from her after we eat. But first, there is something I want to ask her.

She looks surprised and then pleased. "Why not? How about a hot dog?"

We step inside a large tent with a counter and tables. We get our dogs and root beer and sit down.

"Tell me about Father," I begin. I realize right away this doesn't sound right. But she doesn't look too amazed.

"He's coming along, Emily. You can't expect him to change overnight. He is so wrapped up in you. His only child. It's difficult when there is only one. The very idea that you want to go away to college is hard for him to accept."

So that's where we are.

"He didn't try very hard to find my twin," I say. "He wasn't very wrapped up in her."

My "mother's" mouth falls open. "But he did! Whatever

makes you think he didn't try to find Elaine? He spent years sending out detectives all over the country looking for her. Even though he knew she couldn't still be alive. It upsets him to talk about that child. He can't bear it that he lost her." She is glaring at me. Fiercely. This woman has an unfriendly glare.

"He did?" I say.

She nods vigorously. Then solemnly she says, "You've been thinking about this, haven't you?"

"I just don't know why..." I stop. I can't ask her about that. About why he treated my mother so badly. About why he tried to prosecute her innocent friend, Raul's father. About why he called him "scurvy dog." I start again: "I just wonder if he was good to my first mother. Sometimes I think about that."

Again she doesn't look surprised. "You were bound to ask that someday," she says. And the answer is he is going to tell you about this himself. After you turn sixteen."

"What did he do... that he is sorry for now?" I ask.

"I have to let him tell his own story. But I can tell you mine. Remember, Emily, that I love your father. But I almost left him after we had been married a year."

"You did?" Now I am surprised. I thought Emily's parents were Mr. and Mrs. America.

"He was a driven man. His work meant more to him than you or I did. He was good in court. But he could be mean and small at home, to those closest to him. Perhaps I shouldn't say these things to you. You've always idolized him. I don't want to change that."

"Please, go on." She still hesitates. "I can promise you you won't change my feelings toward him," I say truthfully.

"I began to see how he might have been... in his first marriage. I've said too much. Don't ask me anything else." She starts to get up.

"Wait... Mother. How about now? Is he better to you now?" I ask.

"Oh, everything is fine. I had to threaten to leave him and take you with me. He changed, all right! We are important to him now. I would say your father is a fair judge today. And a loving husband and father. Wouldn't you?"

"So, he has changed?" I ask.

"He has changed," she agrees. After a pause she says, "I'm glad we had this talk. Woman to woman. It helps me see that when you grow up and I don't have a child anymore, I'll have a friend."

We look at each other. We both rise at the same time.

"I'll be home soon." I am thinking I might like her for a friend.

"I'll bet you are going to go looking for that blond boy again. Poor Kyle! Well, don't be too long."

I walk to the bus stop. I am hoping Emily has left the barrio. I am also hoping she won't have time for a long talk with her mother tonight. All I need is another lucky day. Or maybe two.

At home I tell my mama what I want to do tomorrow. She shudders, but she doesn't say I can't.

"Be careful, Elaine. We have made our plans. Don't upset them for a swim in a pool. Even though it is by all rights your pool, too."

"But I have to see Dean again, Mama. You saw him with Emily; remember? I have to find out if it is me he likes. You said I couldn't bring anybody here. What can I do?"

"It's taking a chance. But you can't be called a trespasser. So . . . I will give my permission. With one condition: You have to ask somebody else to go swimming with you. You can't meet this boy alone at an empty house."

"But, but . . ." I begin.

"That's it." When my mama makes up her mind, I know it is useless to argue.

I call Ilda. I say I am Emily. I invite her to my house. Bring Scurvy, I tell her. I know she wouldn't come if she knew who I was. Now for Michelle. If she comes to Emily's "pool party," she won't be able to go to the farm and help with the buggy rides. She won't be able to tell Emily she clogged with me. I mean with "her."

I look up her number, call her, and invite her to "my" house for a swim.

"What about Farm Day? What about the buggy rides?" she asks.

"I've got somebody to do it for me. Somebody who knows more than I do about it," I explain. I add recklessly, "Why don't you bring your boyfriend?"

If I am going to get into trouble, it might as well be big trouble.

CHAPTER
TWENTY-ONE

I take a bus uptown and walk the five blocks out to my father's house. I know the address. Three-thirty-seven Hickory Street. But I haven't seen the house.

I look like one of the Mexican or black cleaning women this morning. I have a kerchief tied around my head to hide my hair, and I am carrying a sack. Cleaning women carry sacks as well as purses. The sack is for food handouts to take home to the children. Leftovers from the family table. My sack has food in it but a bathing suit, too.

I've got to get in a better frame of mind. It isn't easy. I am walking along a street of immense green lawns and big two-storied houses. The yardmen are out clipping hedges, and the cleaning women are hustling trash cans out to the curb. Thursday is a big day for cleaning women. We, I mean they, can always get work on Thursday and Friday because people like the Pettys are getting ready for weekend parties.

If I saw my twin coming toward me right now, I'd sock her in the nose.

I must be getting close to the house. Here is three-thirty-five. The next house should be . . . good grief! Did it have to be a mansion?

All I can see from the street is this rise of green grass and banks of azaleas and way, way back, behind some trees, is this roof. But I can tell from glimpses between the trees that my father's house is right out of *Gone With The Wind*.

I sit on the stone wall that curves out with the driveway

and wait. I want to be sure the family is gone. I look at my watch. Nine-thirty. Father goes to work early. He is probably gone already. The public is invited to visit the family farm between ten and three, so "Mother" has to open up out there no later than ten. If she hasn't left already, she will have to leave soon. She and my twin.

Ooops! I hop down off the stone wall and crouch behind it. A car is coming down the driveway. It slows right in front of me, on the other side of the wall. Right on cue, there sits "Mother" in the driver's seat. Emily sits beside her.

The big car pulls out into the street and swooshes away.

I am home free! As they say. I want to run up the driveway, but I make myself walk up. All of a sudden I don't hate this place anymore. Today it is mine!

I pull the kerchief off my hair and let the red stuff tumble down.

I come through a tunnel of overhanging trees. I come out of all this shade, cross a stone courtyard, and go right up to the front of the house. It is so big and so pretty, I almost faint. Three stories! Columns go up to the second floor. Above that, nice windows, no gables. Nothing to make you think "cottage." And all gleaming white with black shutters and silver doorknobs. If those doorknobs aren't sterling, I'll feel cheated.

The front door will be locked, of course, but I go up on the high porch and press my nose to the cut-glass panes to look inside.

The door opens! I almost fall inside with it.

"Why, Emily! I thought you left with your mother." It is a Mexican cleaning woman.

"I, uh, came back. Yeah, I got out of the car at the end of the drive and came back," I say.

"Will you be here for lunch?" she asks.

I raise my sack. I am about to say I brought crackers and cheese. I brought this stuff to serve the kids who are coming over for a swim. But something tells me this wouldn't make sense to the cleaning woman.

"I'll be here. All day," I say.

"I'll fix you some lunch," she says.

"Just a sandwich. Better still, let me help you fix some

sandwiches. I've got some friends coming over for a swim. They might get hungry."

"I'll take care of it. There is a full pantry of party supplies. You have already been a help."

"How did I help?" I want to know. I am inside the entranceway. Standing on a marble floor.

She looks at me, surprised. "Like you always do. Your room is immaculate. I won't have to go near your bedroom or your bathroom." She could be talking to me. My mom says the same thing about my room. She laughs. "Your father's study is another story."

"Messy, huh?"

"It's just paper. Nothing you could call dirty."

We are in one of the parlors. A hall runs between two identical parlors. The tall, arched windows let in the softest, most creamy light imaginable.

The cleaning woman is sort of standing at attention. Is she waiting for me to go somewhere? Like to my room?

It has to be upstairs, doesn't it? I head toward the stairs with a loose and easy walk, glancing back to see the expression on her face. I must be doing all right. I go up. The stairs curve and take me out of her sight. My forehead is wet with sweat. Nervous sweat.

I walk along the upstairs hall pushing doors open. One door opens into a bedroom with a fuzzy navy blue throw rug and a matching polyurethane desk and chair. This could be Emily's. But it looks like the room of a younger person. Why polyurethane? In a Southern mansion! And why so much gray? At once I seem to hear my twin's voice. "It's not me! It's not me!"

I go in and close the door. What have I gotten myself into this time? How will I ever get myself out of it? I want to throw myself on the bed, but it is one of those high ones. I have to crawl up like I'm starting to climb a mountain. I get on it and stretch out.

There is a knock on the door.

I say, "Come in."

It is Michelle.

"Rose told me you were up here. Why aren't you in your bathing suit? Everybody else is in the pool."

"I'm coming, I'm coming," I say. She leaves me to put on my bathing suit.

I love my body. I've got these nice breasts. Not too big. Just right. I always stand very straight to show them off. They are my second favorite part of me. Right after my red hair. If it weren't for my breasts, I think I'd look too thin. My legs are way too long, and I don't have a lot in the hip department. But I walk out straight and proud of myself, right up to the pool.

Dean takes one look and gasps.

"What a great bathing suit," he says.

"It sure beats the big floppy shirt you usually cover up with," Broderick says. He is flexing his mighty shoulders as he gets ready to dive off the diving board.

Scurvy stares, too, and I like it. I am a hog for attention, as I have said before.

Ilda, who is paddling up to the pool edge, says, "Thanks for asking us. We came straight out here like you said. Is that okay?" She seems anxious.

I hate to see her uneasy. I wish I could tell her who I am.

"She was up in her room. Flat on her back. Can you believe it?" Michelle says. "I thought I was going to have to drag her out."

"This was your idea, Emily. You can't get a bunch like us together and then hide," Scurvy says. "Mama says you got in the car with your mother and rode all the way to the end of the driveway before you decided to come back and wait for us."

"Your mother?" I ask.

"You didn't know your cleaning woman was my mother?" he asks.

Broderick makes a sound. I look at him, and I don't like his expression.

"Come on, you guys. Loosen up." I pull Dean by the arm, and we step into the pool. We swim to the other end.

"What's going on?" he asks me when we are on the other side of the pool.

CHAPTER
TWENTY-TWO

Everything seems to be going fine. Everybody is in the pool. We kick, splash, and belly flop off the diving board. Ilda swims like a seal; you just see a flash of her zooming by. Scurvy sinks to the bottom and holds his breath longer than the rest of us. Broderick dives with perfect form. His perfect form stays on the board a lot, so all may view it. Michelle proves it is possible to look beautiful with wet hair.

After a few minutes Dean and I crawl out of the pool and sit on the edge with our feet in the water, holding hands.

"Will we ever be alone?" Dean groans, close to my ear.

We are sitting on the steps at the shallow end of the pool.

"Aren't you having fun?" I ask. But I know what he means.

I look around at "my friends." Ilda and Scurvy are sitting at the umbrella table. Michelle and Broderick are at the back door reaching up for trays of sandwiches Scurvy's mother has just brought out. They bring the trays to the umbrella table and call out, "Chow."

The food is good, and we are all hungry. Dean pours punch into glasses.

"Let's toast somebody," he says. "Let's toast Emily."

"Let's toast her red hair," Scurvy says.

We clink our glasses, too hard, and toss back some punch.

"Let's toast Ilda's big toe," Scurvy says. "She stubbed it

on the stone walk, but it didn't break. It refused to break. A good Mexican toe."

We clink our glasses again and toss back some more punch.

Michelle says, "Let's toast Brod's shoulders. The best shoulders in the county."

Again we do it. I am getting full of punch. I can hear the liquid begin to gurgle around inside me.

"Now what will we toast?" I ask. I am looking at Scurvy. He and Ilda are trying so hard to fit in. I feel for them. I turn away and say, "Let's toast the toast. Scurvy's mother makes the best toasted sandwiches I ever tasted."

We clink again. We drink some more. Everybody except Broderick. Broderick is looking bored. I don't know how I know that. He always looks a little bored to me; it is his natural expression. "Yeah." He rolls his eyes.

Scurvy's voice comes through the general noise. "What's wrong with my mother's sandwiches?" he says to Broderick.

This is ridiculous! "Good grief, Scurvy! Don't be so touchy," I say.

Broderick lumbers backward. "What's the matter with him?" he asks Michelle. "Have I got to eat another dog biscuit to prove they're okay?"

Chairs fall over; feet fly; Ilda and Michelle scream. Scurvy and Broderick are fighting. They push and slap at each other.

Michelle yells, "Stop it! Stop it!" She pulls at Broderick.

"I'm just trying to slap this mosquito off me, for pete's sake. I don't want to hurt him." Broderick is trying to talk through a trickle of blood that seeps from his nose.

Scurvy flies at him again. They are on the edge of the pool. Broderick goes in.

His head surfaces. He spews water, saying, "I'm going to kill the little Mex for that." He heaves himself up on the pool edge.

"No, you're not," I say.

"Come on, Emily. Let me at him. What's it to you? I don't know why you had to ask these people over anyway.

What are you trying to prove? They'll never be like the rest of us, don't you know that? From the day they're born they're a different breed."

"You Neanderthal," I say quietly. "Get out of my yard. Get off of my property. And don't ever come back."

Things grow very quiet. Michelle glares at me as she gathers up Broderick's and her towels. Broderick takes a towel from her and holds it to his nose. They walk toward the house. In a minute I hear Broderick's car start up and drive down the long driveway.

"So. Let's eat," I say. "We don't want to leave all this good food."

Scurvy is still breathing hard. "I'm sorry," he says.

"We should never have come," Ilda says. She turns to me. "Maybe Broderick is right. Maybe we Mexicans don't mix well with other kids. Maybe we shouldn't come to your birthday party."

I groan. If Dean weren't beside me, I would tell Ilda who I am. "You have to come. For all the Mexican kids," I say. I am one of them, I am thinking.

The four of us resume our seats at the table. We munch in silence. Finally Ilda says, "What will your mother think when she hears about this, Emily?"

We all jump up and pick up the fallen chairs. We straighten up the patio.

Actually the party never gets back on its feet. Soon Ilda and Scurvy leave.

"Alone at last," Dean says rather soberly. "It's not quite what I had in mind."

He gets up and bends over my chair. "I didn't want you to be feeling bad; I wanted you feeling good. For our first kiss."

He doesn't have to beg. I lift my face. His mouth comes down and covers mine. It is a cool kiss. Not too exciting. I guess I am more upset than I thought.

I am still thinking about the fight. About the way Broderick talked to Scurvy. The way he said the word *"Mex."* Like it had four letters instead of three. My skin burns at the memory.

What about Dean? How does he feel about Mexicans?

He has drawn his chair up close to mine. He takes my hand.

"I was proud of you, Emily. You are real after all. When I first heard about this house, I didn't know what to expect. I was afraid I had fallen in love with a rich girl who might look down on the rest of us." He pecks me on the cheek. "But you're not like that. Not at all. Lucky me!"

Something he said makes me forget all the rest. He said he had fallen in love with me.

"I love you, too," I say.

He kisses me again. This kiss is not cool.

When we come up for air, I push him away.

"So you found out I am not the typical little rich girl. How would you feel if you found out I am Mexican?"

Did I say something funny? Dean throws his head back and laughs. He bounces back up and puts both hands on his chest and says, "How would you feel if you found out I am Chinese? Wouldn't you love me just the same?" He bends toward me now, sober and intense. "Wouldn't you? Not everybody can be Scotch-English or whatever."

I persist. "What if you found out I wasn't rich?" I suspect he will find this out in the very near future.

"Do we have time for this?" He grows more intense. "Grow up, Emily. I'm not in love with your house, if that's what you mean. There are several hundred just like it in Charleston." He gives me a scorching look. An angry look. "What kind of guy do you think I am?"

I feel like a fool. How could I be so silly?

"Look at me, please." His voice has softened. I look. He murmurs, "I'd love you if you lived in a shack. Okay?"

For answer I take his face in my hands, aim his mouth at mine, and give him a kiss he'll never forget.

When we come apart, I say, "What if you found out my name isn't Emily?" I say, softly.

He walks me up the path to the little shack in the barrio my mother and I have rented. He comes in to meet Mama.

I feel so good, I am beaming all over. I go outside to kiss him good night. Now he knows he's kissing me, Elaine!

"How am I going to know you Saturday night?" he asks anxiously. I am meeting him at the Halloween Street Dance uptown. Everyone will be in costume. Everyone will be wearing a mask. "I'm sure your twin is great, but I don't want any more mix-ups. Please, Elaine. Make it foolproof. The next time I kiss a redhead I want to be sure it is you."

"You'll know. I'll see to that," I tell him. I am hugging him hard. I hate to let him go. This is only Thursday. Saturday night seems like a long time away. But Mama and I must talk.

The sun is going down. My mother is holding a backpack toward me. She wants me to strap it on her back. Night is on the way, and my mother wants to go to a strange, woodsy place and walk twenty miles in the dark. I am horrified.

"Are you sure you want to do this?" I ask.

She peers back at me as I work on the catch to the backpack. She doesn't say anything.

"Oh, all right. But please be careful," I say.

She smiles her wonderful, wide smile. "I knew you'd understand. I can't wait any longer. To be with Emily. Even as a stranger. I will listen. I know she will talk to me. Night is conducive. The dark will cover us. I will put my bedroll beside her and sleep next to her. Think of it, Elaine!"

She is sooo happy! It makes me feel good to see her this way. The years of separation from her other child have been hard. For me, too.

I have thought of my missing twin every day of my life. I have heard her voice in my dreams. I have never felt she was far away. I long to be with her.

Especially now that I know we won't be fighting over Dean!

"I wish I were going with you," I moan. "I wish I could see Emily tonight."

Mama gives me a steely look. Her lower lip protrudes, and her small jaw sticks out. "It won't be long now. My girls will soon be together."

CHAPTER
TWENTY-THREE

It is Friday morning. My mother has come back from her overnight hike as happy as I have ever seen her. She is now asleep on the couch where she sat down to rest "for just a minute."

I slip out of the house. I have one more thing to do on my own.

I enter my father's waiting room. I have brought someone with me. The two of us walk straight to my father's private office door, and after a light knock we go in.

"Emily! This is getting to be a habit. I like it. Why... you've brought a friend." The judge gets up from behind his desk, comes around it, and reaches to shake Raul's hand. Raul withdraws his hand as soon as it is shook.

My father turns to me. He gives me a kiss on the cheek. "How was the overnight hike?" he asks. I say something agreeable, and he returns to his chair. With his desk between us I feel like he has put something else between us. He is surprised to see Raul. And he is wary.

"Is this a social visit, or is it business?" he asks lightly, looking at Raul.

Raul and I are sitting in chairs facing the judge's desk. Raul leans forward and laces his fingers.

"I need to know who is taking care of my father's grave. Every time I go out there to rake leaves, it is already done."

"And you think I can tell you?" my father asks him.

Raul looks at me. He didn't want to come. "Father," I

begin, "Raul's mother says you are paying for her to go to night school. She says you are going to pay for Raul's college. Don't you think you ought to tell Raul what is going on? He is eighteen. He'll graduate this spring." I keep my voice as pleasant as possible. No screaming, I say to myself. We had enough of that at the pool yesterday.

"It's true, I am doing those things. I am paying for your mother's secretarial training. I'd like to have her work here in the office instead of at the house. I am also paying for the upkeep of your father's grave, Raul. And I will pay for your college." My father's blue eyes are not twinkling.

His expression is determinedly businesslike.

I like his attitude.

Raul has turned a deep red. What now?

"I don't think you should do those things unless we ask you . . . and we haven't asked you," he says.

"I'll do exactly what I think I should do. I don't have to be asked, nor do I have to ask anybody." The judge's wrinkled face is hard. His lips are set.

Raul stands up. "You can't pay for what you did. There is no way—"

My father interrupts him. "I know that. Give me credit. I am not trying to buy my way into heaven, Raul. You young fellows have just one way of looking at people like me. We are money-grubbers. Or," he throws out a hand, "we are the oppressors of the poor. Right?" He waits.

Raul puts his hands on his hips and glares. But he doesn't speak. I think my dad has hooked him. He has definitely got his attention.

Dad stands up. He is short, but he seems to grow. He leans over the desk toward Raul. "Do you get up at four every morning? No. I did. Every day. I worked my father's groves. Like a dog. I have worked every day of my life to get where I am. It's true I had certain advantages. Such as I am trying to give you. Like college. A lot of fellows of my time didn't get to college. It was a big thing for us. And I appreciated it.

"I have apologized to your mother for the way I treated your father. I apologize to you for that. I was a young fool to call him names. In his case I should have listened to my betters. But I didn't kill him; I prosecuted the man who did." He leans back more relaxed. "I can't do anything about that now. You can accept my apology or not, as suits your fancy. But if you refuse to go to college when you've got the chance, then I will think you are as big a fool as I was."

I can't help myself. I admire that judge. I don't care if he is my own father.

Raul sits down. "My mother told me it would be like this." He looks at me. "I'm ready to go when you are."

We all stand up. Dad nods at Raul. There is no hand-shaking this time.

I go behind the desk and kiss that hard, mean little guy, my father, on the top of the head. His blue eyes pop wide open. He looks up at me in wonder.

"Raul is bringing his girlfriend to my birthday party" I warn.

"Good," says the judge.

Raul and I get to the door. Raul turns. Looking at my father, he mutters a small "thank you" and goes out.

I smile back at my old man. He returns my smile.

When I get home, Mama and I go into a huddle. We go over our final plans. Once, twice, three times. And some-thing tells me, we'll be adding details later as the time draws near.

CHAPTER
TWENTY-FOUR

Mama and I were supposed to have a long, leisurely day today. It is Friday.

We sack out all afternoon. I have been too visible, Mama tells me. We are extremely lucky we haven't been discovered. No more risk taking, she advises.

I talk to Dean on the telephone. I wish I could be with him. He says the wait is killing him.

Late in the afternoon, when I am flopped in a chair with a book almost asleep, I sense Emily's presence. She is here in the barrio! I know it. I slip out of the house. The sun is low, so I stay in the long shadows cast by the buildings, and soon I am at the back door of the stockroom. As soon as I step inside I see Kyle.

He doesn't see me. He is bent over his endless inventory papers. I walk lightly along behind the barrels of beans and edge up to the door leading to the Exchange. I hear my twin's voice. Then I hear Ilda answer her.

Emily is saying she is mad at her father. She is so angry she never wants to see him again. She knows now about the divorce and the custody trial. She can't bear to go back home. Not tonight. She asks Ilda if she can spend the night with her. I wait just long enough to hear Ilda say yes, then I go home as quietly and as quickly as I can. I lay an idea on my mother that makes her crazy.

The idea is so good and so scary, we are both nervous wrecks just talking about it.

Finally she agrees, shivering and hugging me and warning me to be careful.

* * *

I am back in the stockroom hiding again. Kyle finishes his work and goes into the Exchange. I creep up to the Exchange door and wait until he tells Emily good night. I am out of the stockroom's back door and around in the front of the building in a flash. I slow down. I look down at my clothes. Like Emily I am wearing blue jeans, but my shirt is blue instead of gray. I hope he won't notice. In the twilight I can just see Kyle picking up his bicycle. I saunter up to him as casually as I can.

"Time to get home," I say. My voice is too high, but maybe he won't notice.

"You're going home? After all that?" He has straddled his bike and is standing there looking amazed.

"Yeah. I decided I'd better," I say, getting on Emily's bike. I wish we could get past the talk and move. I glance back at the Exchange. Nobody comes out.

"Come on," I call, riding down the road to the highway.

He rides up alongside me. "I can't believe you changed your mind so soon. I thought you'd never speak to your dad again. That's what you said."

"I've got to sooner or later. I'm trying to be realistic," I say.

He shakes his head, and we ride in silence.

When we get to town, he turns up Hickory Street, and I follow, glad one of us can remember the way in the almost-dark. We stop at the driveway, and before he can lean over for a kiss I say good-bye and zoom up toward the house.

The Petty house.

"Hello, Mother," I say quietly. I know Emily has quarreled with her parents. I've got to get into the role, my sister's role.

The woman rushes toward me, arms out. I am in for a big hug.

"We were so worried. You didn't say where you were going." She leans back from me. "Did you know it's nearly eight o'clock?" The fierce scowl comes on. "Where's your watch?"

My father comes out into the entranceway where we are standing. He gives me a chilly nod. "I thought I heard voices. Where have you been? You had your mother worried."

"Just riding around." I know I am too placid. Emily wouldn't be like this. She would still be mad. She still is mad. I stiffen up. "If you'll excuse me, I'm going to my room," I say, lift my chin, and sail away toward the staircase. I love exits.

As I climb out of their sight with the curve of the staircase, I hear my "mother" say "She didn't eat her supper!"

I find Emily's room and escape inside. Whew!

First I flop on the bed to recover from the strain this charade is putting on me. Then I get up and look around. I push a door. A dressing room full of girl clothes. My colors, too. Just like me, Emily likes to wear bright colors. So why is this room the color of a grave? Coordinated with the color of a rainy day?

I push open another door. The bathroom. A big bathroom. As big as my bedroom at home. And, get this, a Jacuzzi takes up about half of this bathroom.

I yelp with delight. I throw my clothes off and get in. Soon I've got the Jacuzzi full of beautiful sudsy water all the way up to my chin.

"Oh, here you are!" It is my "mother." Not even a knock. Just barges in. She lowers the toilet seat and makes herself at home. "I've been thinking about your hair."

What now? I reach up and feel a long slimy-wet strand of my hair.

"Like you said the other day, it's not too bright. And now that you've decided you like it the natural color, we won't have to tone it down anymore." She smiles brightly.

"Right," I say.

"But how would you like to get it cut? There is a very good stylist downtown, a man who has just been hired at the beauty salon. He does a wonderful job. Did you notice my new cut?" She swings her head around.

"Get my hair cut?" I ask.

"Styled. So it's not so shaggy," she says.

I look at this woman. She sits straight back on Emily's gray toilet seat. She is tense as a cat on a hunt. Nervous. Her big eyes are glaring down at me. What goes on?

"I don't think so, Mother. I like my hair long. And

shaggy." I say this patiently. She turns gray to match the decor. She looks old. I add, "But maybe we can think of something. Something to do to my hair that we will both like." I realize I like Kay, this "mother" of Emily's. I don't like to see her worried or upset. I hope I am saying something that will make her smile.

She hangs her head. She puts both hands to her face. What goes on?

I get out of the Jacuzzi and wrap a giant towel around myself.

"What's the matter?" I ask, bending over her.

She is crying. "I don't know," she wails.

I sort of hug her from a standing position.

"Mother," I say, "let's move into the bedroom." I go ahead of her and walk into the dressing room, where I find a nightie hanging on a hook. I'm in it and out. "Mother" is now sitting on that enormous bed. She is dry-eyed.

"I'm not one of these women who has stayed at home all her life. I have always had outside interests. But when you go away to college . . ." She stops and looks at me, but I only nod agreement. She goes on: "When you go away to college, I will miss you. I will miss doing things for you." She stops again. "Maybe I have been doing things to you instead of for you, but I did the best I could."

"I think you must have done a pretty good job. Em . . . I mean, I look great, don't I? No pointed head. No bruised egos. Everything turned out great. Except the colors in this room. Ugh!"

She gasps. "You don't like the colors? Why didn't you tell me?"

"Did you do them? I mean, why didn't you ask me before you did them?" I ask.

She brightens. "We'll start over. We'll do this whole room over. I'll bring home my catalogs of colors, drapery, furniture, the whole bit. And you can pick out exactly what you want." She is smiling. This woman is pretty! Really good-looking.

"Sounds good. But can it wait a day or two? I'm pooped. I know it's early, but I'm going to bed," I say.

"My poor darling! I've kept you up. Let Mother tuck you in."

I have to submit. I crawl up on the big bed and let her pull the covers over me. Then she bends down and pecks me on the forehead. When she gets to the door, I call "I love you, Mother. Good night."

I don't know why I said that. I think I said it for Emily. It was like her voice came through my mouth. It was like she wanted that said at that time. Or would have if she had been here. Even though she is with our mama tonight, I know she loves "Mother," too.

I jump out of bed and push the door closed. I am on my way back to the bed when I notice a hand mirror on Emily's vanity. I pick it up and take it with me.

I sit cross-legged in the middle of the bed on top of the coverlet. Lotus position. Dancers like to sit this way. It feels good. Keeps us limber.

I study my face in the mirror. Anybody's face is a little peculiar. All that activity going on. Breathing, snuffling, sneezing. Eyes rolling around in their sockets. Tongue licking lips. Mouth swallowing. How can this add up to a face? A thing you have to present to the world. The part of you everybody sees all the time?

On the other hand I like mine. My face. My nose is perfect. My eyes are absolutely gorgeous. But my ears . . . I pull the hair back and expose my ears. My terrible secret! They are elephant ears. Big, fat, and unattractive. Short hair? Never!

I really am tired. And it's not all that early anymore. I crawl under the covers and plump up my pillow. My hand touches something under the pillow.

I pull the something out. It is a rag doll.

I can't believe my twin sleeps with a baby's doll. But what else is this doll doing here?

I am sitting up holding the doll in front of me. Out of nowhere that doll's name comes to me. Edith!

"Edith!" I whisper aloud. I hug the doll up to my breast. I am filled with a jumble of feelings. I try to sort them out. I say the doll's name again: "Edith!"

In my head I hear voices. "Give her to me! Give me; give me!" It is my sister's voice . . . and mine. One on top of the other. We are fighting, pulling at Edith, jerking the doll this way and that.

I sit and hold Edith for a long time. Listening to those baby voices in my head. I feel close to Emily. I can almost reach out and touch her. Then I crawl back under the covers with Edith in my arms and go to sleep.

CHAPTER
TWENTY-FIVE

The next morning is Saturday. It is Halloween, the last day of the Festival. I eat breakfast with my solemn parents. Dad then goes into his study, and my mother dresses to go to the Pioneer Craft Fair.

"You are coming, aren't you, Emily?" she asks.

"Is Dad staying home?" I want to know.

"Yes. All the offices are closed today. Everybody is going to the craft fair. Don't you remember?" she says.

"Will you be gone long?" I ask.

"If you aren't going with me, I'll just breeze uptown and be home for an early lunch. Do you want to eat on the patio? We're fixing our own lunch today, so we can make it simple."

"I'll make some sandwiches and have them ready," I say.

The morning is chilly, but it warms up fast. I sunbathe and take a dip in the pool. What a life! Now to the kitchen. By twelve I have a platter stacked high with crazy sandwiches, the kind I make at home—figs, peanut butter, and cream cheese mashed up together for the filling. On very thin rye. I also make a pitcher of mixed cranberry and pink grapefruit juice. When everything is set up outside, I cover the food to keep the insects out. But I don't have long to wait.

Mother comes out, bringing my father with her. She is pulling him around by the arm like she does me. He allows it.

I let them eat first. I don't want to spoil their lunch. Then after they eat they look peaceful and sleepy, and I don't want to give them indigestion. I'll bet this kind of thinking is what got Emily into trouble with her parents. They aren't the kind of people who take shocks very well. But I have to upset them sooner or later.

"Mother, Father," I begin. That sounds so ominous they both sit straight up, stiff-backed in their patio chairs.

"You have been good to me. I want to break this to you as easily as I can." That gets their attention.

"First, Dad, you have to promise me the custody battle is over. And will never be brought up again," I say, looking him right in the eye.

The parents turn to each other. Their mouths have dropped open. Father turns back to me.

In a bare whisper he says, "You've heard something. About Elaine."

I don't deny it. He tries to get up but falls back in his chair. "For God's sake, Emily! If you have heard something about my . . . child." His voice goes faint. He seems to be choking.

I ignore this heart attack he seems to be having.

"First, you have to promise me the custody battle is buried." I like it when I get tough. It feels good. "Your daughters are young women now. It is too late to fight over us. We will decide our own future."

Kay gets up and stands over Father. She feels his head like a mother does a child with a fever. She looks up at me, not scowling. Pleading with her big eyes.

I wait.

"I promise," my father says.

"Elaine is alive and well," I say sweetly. This is fun!

Father sits up, and Kay goes back to her chair. She can't seem to sit down. She stands beside it.

Father's blue eyes are glistening. The man has tears in his eyes! My heart aches for him. If I could just be sure . . . he won't give my mother any trouble, I would . . . love him so much.

"I always knew if any news ever came, it would come to you," he says weakly. "My dear Emily. Believe me. I want nothing more than to see my lost baby again."

"She's not a baby anymore, Father," I warn again.

"You've seen her?" He jumps up. He bends over me. I have to stand up to get him to back off.

"A year from now we will both be living on a college campus. I hope we go to the same college. I hope you will finance both of us. Maybe, if you don't buy the car . . ."

"Please, Emily. For God's sake! Tell me where my other child is. Tell me I can see her. Tell me she doesn't hate me."

I reach out my arms. I make my face as open as I can. I make it say "Here she is," but I don't speak. I can't. Suddenly I've got a lump in my throat as big as Stone Mountain.

Something in my father's face changes. His eyes go wide. I think he is catching on. I swallow the big, hard lump.

I say "I am Elaine."

CHAPTER
TWENTY-SIX

It is wonderful to be held in my father's arms. Not as Emily. As me. We hang onto each other.

I hear someone crying and glance at Kay.

"I am so happy for you!" she says.

We are in the middle of the scene I have dreamed of all my life when suddenly everybody goes crazy.

First Kay gets up on her feet with a stagger. "Then where is Emily?" she says with a quaver.

Next Dad backs off and says "Where is she?" He looks around the patio like she might be under a chair.

Both of them stare at me. I tell them as simply as I can that Emily is at the barrio. She spent the night.

Now they run around bumping into each other. "Get the car out," one says. The other says, "You get the car out. I'll get our jackets." Then the other one says, "Forget the jackets; it's warm. Just hurry!"

I have to tell them "Sit down!"

They stop in their tracks.

"Please sit down," I say again. "Emily is with her mother. For the first time in twelve years. She isn't going to leave. Not for a while. They need some time."

The parents sit down. Or fall down in their chairs again. This time they say absolutely nothing.

"It's not as bad as you think," I tell my father. "Mama wants us to meet them at the street dance tonight. Then she is staying over until next week. For our sixteenth birthday. After that she is going to swap kids with you again; I am going back to California, and Emily is coming home. We both have high school to finish."

The parents sag in their chairs. They are still pale, but they look relieved.

"But . . . when do I get to have you stay with us, Elaine?" Dad asks.

"We want to visit back and forth. Often. Together. I'll come here and stay with Emily and you. And Emily can come stay with Mama and me. Whenever you say. Whenever we can."

"Two girls in the house! Oh, how wonderful!" Kay leans forward in her chair. "I'll fix up one of the guest rooms. Let's see, which one? Maybe the one next to Emily's room. That way I could use gray throughout . . ." She catches my eye. "Better still, I'll wait until you two are both here, and we'll fix up the second bedroom together. That is, if you don't mind sharing Emily's room until your own bedroom is ready?" she asks timidly.

"I like it!" I cry. I like the whole picture. I can't wait to get back to California to brag about this place. I do a fast clog, throw my arms up, and spin around. I come to a perfect stop in a deep curtsy.

The parents clap. It is a wan little clap. But I can see they are reviving.

"Now," I say, "we have to plan tonight."

CHAPTER
TWENTY-SEVEN

The little town of Fern, Florida, is dark tonight. The streetlights are turned off. Lanterns, hundreds of them, have been strung on wires everywhere. Their dusky glow is pretty, but they don't give much light. That is the way it is supposed to be. This is Halloween, the night of the Pioneer Festival's Street Dance.

Dad tells me the city fathers (and mothers) have been stringing lanterns around the square for Halloween since my great-grandmother's day. I didn't know I could get interested in Fern's history, but I have. I am not just Mexican, after all. I am half–Scotch-English, like Fern herself.

I am walking between my Father and Kay. Like everybody else we are completely disguised. Our old-fashioned costumes and masks hide our identities.

"This is fun!" Kay says.

I think she is saying it for Dad. He is almost in a coma over what is going to happen. At last he is going to see his two children together again. And he is going to see his first wife, too. I guess this is pretty heavy stuff.

"You look great," I tell him. He is wearing a kid's costume. It fits him perfectly. When we rented costumes this afternoon, nothing in the men's line fit him. I have to say he looks adorable in his Pinocchio vest, shirt, and knee breeches. He didn't notice. He didn't look in a mirror. He just said "Let's go" and followed us out to the car like a zombie.

I hope he'll snap out of it before we find Mama and Emily.

Kay looks fine. She chose a chimney sweep costume. She is stalking ahead of us, carrying a short black broom. I grab the tail of her suit to slow her down.

I am dressed as a male mariachi dancer. This costume is part of my mother's plan. She wanted to be able to recognize me in the crowd. She and Emily are dressed as mariachi dancers also, with Mama as the woman and Emily dressed exactly like me.

Emily! I can't believe the time has come. I am going to see my sister. My twin. My throat feels funny. Like I can't swallow for a second. I must stay calm.

Maybe Emily will see me before I see her. Tonight we can't look for red hair. Our hair is up under our mariachi hats.

We promenade once completely around the courthouse square, pushing through the festival crowd. There is not the usual roar of talk tonight. Tonight the crowd is murmuring, whispering. It's more spooky that way.

"Aren't the children wonderful?" Kay says. "Look at that rosebush?"

We watch a little kid dressed as a full-blooming rosebush go waddling by. She opens a path through the thick of the crowd, and a gaggle of geese follow her, squawking and hissing. Not real geese; more kids, of course.

We stop and step off the path and watch as teenage warlocks storm through. Devils with long forked tails run after them. A unicorn is next and then a whole family of Dickens characters followed by Ilda and Raul dressed as Romeo and Juliet. I think I see Michelle and Broderick. I'm not sure. But a Henry the Eighth and one of his headless wives passes close enough to touch. The headless wife speaks to me (through the front of a tall collar) in, I think, Michelle's voice.

"Dean is behind us," the wife says in a loud whisper. Her hand brushes mine. I am glad she isn't mad at me. I mean at "Emily."

I forget my poor father. I rush up to Dean, who is wearing a harlequin costume. I mean, I do love the guy, but I could get used to him in a hurry if he wore that costume every day. What a body! No big bumpy muscles anywhere; just smooth and elegant all over.

We grab hands and kiss. Just a peck. I promise to look

for him when the Street Dance begins, and then I send him off. I turn around to go back to my dad and Kay and come face-to-face with Kyle.

Kyle is a hangman. Hatchet and all! This guy is one of a kind.

"I thought I'd never find you, Emily. Why didn't you tell me how you were going to dress?" Without waiting for an answer he gives me a hug. "Guess what? I won the song competition. My alligator song . . . it won!" I dodge a kiss and start talking to ward off another kiss. The trouble is I like him. Why wouldn't I? He is my twin sister's guy.

"That's great, Kyle. Just great." A song about an alligator?

I make excuses and get away from the guy as fast as I can. I don't love anybody but Dean, but with Kyle . . . watch out. The chemistry is there.

Maybe this is what happened between Emily and Dean. Emily and I, we've got a problem, but it sounds like more fun than trouble.

I am back beside my dad and Kay. They have been chatting with a beautiful Cleopatra. The black woman. She is wearing a half mask that lets her Egyptian skin show.

Her Julius Caesar, a man swathed in bedsheets, bows to me. "This girl is good in the kitchen," he says. "She can order the best pizza you ever tasted." Everybody smiles. Me, too. I like it when Emily gets compliments.

"It won't be long now," I tell the parents. "My mother is never late."

I hardly finish speaking when she walks up to us. I think I am going to have to hold Dad up by the arms.

Mama removes her mask. She looks like she always looks. Beautiful. Mama throws out a hand. "Hello, Wesley."

Dad's hand hangs in the air. She takes it and shakes it.

"Is it Evita?" he asks. After a moment he straightens up and says, "Hello, Evita. It's been a long time." They look at each other, a little puzzled. This is a strange moment for all of us. At last Dad and Mama smile, and Dad introduces Kay. The two women shake hands. Timidly. Determinedly cordial.

I have been really worried about this meeting. My mind has been totally on my father and mother. Suddenly I whirl around. Where is she? Where is she? Am I looking the wrong way? I turn again and almost bump into another male mariachi dancer. About my height. Exactly my height.

I start to tremble. My teeth chatter. I hope nobody hears.

I am so close to this other dancer I could touch her on the nose. I don't have to look behind me to know all three parents are watching. And waiting.

The person in front of me moves closer. She peers into my mask. I think I hear her teeth chattering, too.

This feels like a dream. I must come out of it. I reach up and take off my mask.

The mask in front of me comes off.

There is that face. My face. On someone else. A thrill shoots through me. I can hardly breathe.

It feels like my blood is on fire.

Trembling, I reach up and take hold of Emily's hat. She stands still. I take the hat off her head.

The red hair comes tumbling down. I gasp. Emily reaches up and removes my hat. We stare. The whole world stops. I don't know how long. Finally Emily puts a hand in her pants pocket. She pulls out two combs. They look like my lost hair combs. Without a word she holds them out to me.

I take one, pull my hair back from my face, and tuck the comb in it.

Emily pulls her hair back from her face. She can't get the comb in just right. I reach up. My hand is on hers. Together we push the comb into her hair.

Behind us the Street Dance begins. A wild, thumping rock beat fills the air.

At the same instant we grab each other's hands. At the same instant we say each other's names: "Emily!" "Elaine!"

We do a tug-of-war, laughing and screaming and flinging our heads back to see our parents. Yes, they are right there. You couldn't budge them with a shovel.

I look into that other face.

The other me.

I love her.

About the Author

Charlotte St. John is a professional illustrator as well as a writer, with Masters degrees in both Art and Psychology. A native Floridian, she and her husband currently live in a Vermont-like house in a Florida swamp. They have three children. RED HAIR is the author's third novel, following SHOWDOWN (Fawcett, October 1987) and FINDING YOU (Fawcett, June 1985).

Teens

learn to make tough choices and the meaning of responsibility in novels by **Marilyn Levy**